To Mary Jo~

2014

Abby

Moving Day:
A Season of Letters

Moving Day:

A Season of Letters

A Novel by

Ibby Greer

Brunswick

Library of Congress Cataloging-in-Publication Data
Greer, Elizabeth (Ibby) Taylor, 1950-
  Moving day: a season of letters : a novel / by Ibby Greer.
  -- 1st ed.
    p. c.m.
    ISBN 1-55618-190-6 (cloth : alk. paper)
    1. Women poets--Fiction. 2. Aged women--Fiction.
  3.Widows--Fiction. I. Title.

  PS3557.R3993 M68 2000
  813'.6--dc21   00–045513

This is a work of fiction. Some of the places are real. Except for historical people, all characters are fictitious. The fiction of Ann Bow is her own.

First Edition
Published in the United States of America
by

Brunswick Publishing Corporation
1386 Lawrenceville Plank Road
Lawrenceville, Virginia 23868
1-800-336-7154

This novel is dedicated to my parents,
Elizabeth Bunn Taylor and the late
Henry Stryker Taylor, who instilled in
me a love for letter-writing, travel, and
all things beautiful.

Elise Parker
Ramsey View
Unit 6 R
Monte Vista, AZ 85324

                              Saturday, December 4
Dear Elise,

There is a lot happening here, and you're the one I like to tell first: holiday preparations, the first big snow (but I'm not housebound), Lilla's newfound bitchiness, Ian's condo at Vail. Elise, I'm just plain wondering if you still like it down there, our white Rockies replaced by gold Huachucas: a dry brown land, probably more like Christmas in the Holy Land than up here, isn't it? I remember being in Tucson one winter for a conference Sam attended. Indian pottery, silver, pima cotton, and heat, always the heat. But I'm more conscious of that now, sitting here with ice on the window while you are on some patio sipping margaritas!

The sidewalk is so icy that I had to use my new boots, with the cleats, when I walked down the Hill awhile ago to take my Holiday Letter to the printer. I was able to stride right along with the college students. Bundled up in my old blue duffel coat and plaid scarf, with my white hair covered up, I looked as young as they did, or so I thought. But who cares! The Letter does not say much this year. News, I mean. Remember how I used to include tidbits about world events? I'd try to share a few highlights of the past year, a conference, a walk for ecology, a poetry reading, a particularly good lecture at the university? Well, I don't do that so much anymore. Even if the events in the world stir me, somehow most of the people I have left to me seem to take a dimmer interest in big issues than I do. The ladies in this building, who, as you know, are almost all widows except for the occasional graduate student, would rather talk about a local ordinance against dogs than to discuss something like the kinds of self-imposed problems colleges have because their athletes can't write or read well. I started to mention a coach, who gets paid more than any faculty member has, and before I even started, Miriam O'Hara jumped in and exclaimed about her new "Coach" catalogue! It took me a few seconds to shift my thought, until I realized she was discussing a leather purse!

What are the people like at Ramsey View? I suppose you can't generalize, of course. But, do you find many people like you there? You know that when I say "like you," I mean, also "like me." You have told me a little about some of the people there, where they moved from, what they like to do with their time. I guess I'm asking you whether they do things together, or stay by themselves; whether they tend to dine together in the dining room, or eat alone in their apartments; whether they are gossips or idea-people. Is there a real variety of residents, Elise? Are most of them from the same part of the country? Are there some professional people who have retired there? Or are most of them ladies, such as I, who have dabbled in many things but really never had a "real" career? I ask because I find myself more and more in a minority, I think, of persons who value reflection, careful speech, and ideas, more than I value being passively entertained. Doesn't that sound righteous?! Whoops! I don't play bridge. I don't enjoy a cocktail hour. If one lives at a place like Ramsey View, does one feel compelled to conform??

So many people today seem so very careless about so many things: how they use (abuse) language, their manners, their dress. Imagine someone our age wearing a baseball cap backwards! They argue over "gender bias" and rework all sorts of historic documents in English, but they don't know how to use an adverb! I find it so frustrating. I want to be able to surround myself again with people like me. I am becoming a kind of "dinosaur," aren't I? My kind of educated woman, of the WWII era, is becoming as scarce as our dear veterans. We should have a special monument to women of our era.

With you in Arizona, and my children scattered, and Sam gone, I turn more and more to writing, to listening, and to Sam's music. I am alone, by choice, a great deal of the time. But that is how I like it. I am not sure how I would adapt to a place humming with people meeting each other for dinner or an outing. I want to follow your days at Ramsey View, Elise, so I can better decide if I might wish to make a change, myself, before long. My children are after me to make such a move! You would not have moved to Ramsey View if you had not thought you would like it there. I moved from my house to this apartment almost a decade ago, and I hoped that would be my last move ... or so I try to convince my family. Yet, we are isolated at our age. We become sages or eccentrics, don't we, to those who think they understand us? Our real friends know who we are. Do I want to move? Help me think it through for me; I tire of the subject, but Charles and Lilla cannot get enough of it. I'd rather not go into her moods now ... it will just depress me. (I promise the world: I AM a tolerant mother-in-law.) And I have spent the better part of the day rising above thoughts that would pull me down.

I still have one good friend here in the building: Edwina Kohl. She moved here right after you left town. I don't know if I've mentioned her in any detail, or not. (I know I repeat myself endlessly, Elise, in all my letters ... and it's kind of you not to notice.) She is called Wincey. She has the most extraordinary personality, shot through with gold filaments, so that her conversation glimmers, with anecdotes and memories, illustrated as often as not by sepia-colored photos or etchings kept in a hatbox. (Another person with closets full of filled boxes. Joy!) I find her company soothing, even though she hardly ever sits still. Wincey is joining me this afternoon for tea here. (Irish Afternoon Tea and water-cress/cream cheese sandwiches). You know that my Faye has started a little catering company out of their house in Florida? She just sent me a lovely basket of loose teas, ginger cookies, and nut preserves. Wincey is originally from Vienna. Before the War, you know. And she does love an elegant coffee hour or tea-time. And it gives me a chance to use the Coalport set that you and Bill gave us some thirty years ago. Not a chip in it yet.

You will get my Holiday Letter soon. It is green type on cream paper this year, with a packet of herb tea in each envelope. I do so enjoy writing everyone. And I think my friends have come, over the years, to anticipate my Holiday Letters. I say that because I get no Christmas cards until everyone on my list has received mine and had a chance to answer it! I'm flattered! Oh, how I wish you were going to be up here this year. We miss you. But I know that Arizona will satisfy your dreams. Remember me when you look north. I'm always here for you. As this is your first holiday since Bill passed away, dear one, do your best, and know that I know only too well how empty time can feel without your husband to share things with.

Call me sometime, Elise, if you are up to a chat. I hardly ever use my phone. The children beg me to call more. But I just get their answering machines! On my dime. So I write them. And they write back. Much more civilized, don't you think? And someday, if my hearing goes the way of my dear mother's, when she was in her late 80s, then no one will expect me to phone. My letters will suffice, for I am my letters.

Cheers,

Annie

* * *

Twila Aguirrez-Lomas
Reservation Desk
Flatiron Walk
2298 34th Avenue
Boulder, CO 80302-1298

Ann Cunningham Bow
Dover Terrace # 10
26 Dover Lane
Boulder, CO 80302

Monday, December 6

Dear Ms. Aguirrez-Lomas:

Thank you for your very prompt response to my enquiry concerning the exact dates for the vacation involving my family. I wanted to reconfirm that they have the three suites. My son, Charles Bow, two adults and two teenagers from Ohio, will arrive at mid-day on December 22nd. They would prefer the three-bedroom suite. My daughter Alicia Montgomerie and her son from Massachusetts would like a small, one-bedroom suite, one bath, no special amenities. Her sister and family, Faye and Austin Wills, arriving from Florida on December 23rd, will take a larger one-bedroom suite, hopefully one overlooking the mountains. These are very similar accommodations, I believe, to the ones that I reserved two years ago for the same people. Forgive me for asking on such very short notice. My son has asked if there will be a wet bar in their suite? And my daughter-in-law, Mrs. Bow, wishes to know if there are valet service, a kitchenette in the children's suite, and a hot-tub in their own.

Thank you again for arranging all this. How lucky we were to have the families from Colombia cancel like that! I know that my children and grandchildren will be delighted with Flatiron Walk, as they were last time. The metro service from there to downtown was a real blessing (for me!) Have a pleasant holiday.

Sincerely,

Ann C. Bow

P.S. I will be sending poinsettias closer to their arrival. Could you see, please, that they will be put in the rooms?

* * *

Mrs. Leyman Carter   Ann C. Bow
4123 Cedar Lane   Dover Terrace #10
Boulder, CO 80302   26 Dover Lane

Dec. 6
Dear Mrs. Carter:

I regret that I will be unable to speak at your December meeting this year. I just learned that my family is planning to visit here for the holidays, and I think it would be too much for me to try to do a reading on Wednesday, the 22nd. I do apologize for not being able to tell you this sooner, but I did not know, myself. However, I do thank you for thinking of me again this year. And I may be able to suggest several other people to do a program of some sort for your group, if you would like to have their names. I believe that the children's book illustrator, May Blanding, might be able to speak. Or perhaps James Thompson could read from his new collection of poems about Scandinavia. They are both most pleasant, and like to participate in events in the community. Perhaps you have already met them?

Would you be able to use me sometime later on, perhaps in March or April? In February, I have another library commitment that involves much planning, and I know that I will be pretty busy preparing for that event. Just let me know, if you will, and I will be happy to help. We do not have to use either the main library or the children's library, of course, if you would prefer another location. The reason I am so partial to that library is that I love sitting by the glass walls over the creek.

Best Wishes,

Ann C. Bow

* * *

Dr. Trevor Bowleston
3000 Silver Lode Tower
Suite 24
Denver, CO 80222

Landlord? And surgeon?
Absentee at both?
Or are we, here, the privileged ones?
No need to know who I am.
Are all the elderly invisible?
Or, perhaps, are all absentee owners blind?
I just live here. I rent this air, this view,
From you.
Everyone at Dover Terrace has a cat, or two.
Don't change the rules now, doctor.
We'll just ignore you.

An unhappy tenant

* * *

HOLIDAY LETTER

Dear Friends, a glorious, glorious Holiday:
I have my view across white roofs towards my former
home;
I have had forty years of Boulder snows, yet I'm not
moving. No.
I am surrounded by birdseed, pine needles, stars, my
Sam's music for flute
and classical guitar, "Songs for Silver Plume,"
(on a new Chinook Wind CD playing softly in my room)

and my Russian Blue, Melodie, on the wide windowsill,

avidly watching her birds at the feeders below.

The family won't be here this season, alas.

Alicia continues with Bevel and Bevel in Boston.

David, 12, is thinking about a boarding school.

Charles and Lilla are still in Columbus. And their
daughter Carson, 14,

has become quite a ballerina.

Their son Adam, 12, apparently excels in video games. (?)

My baby, Faye, and her husband Austin continue to enjoy
Florida.

Faye has started a catering company called "High Tea."

She also mails custom-made baskets of gourmet delights.

(Give her a call: 561-HIG-HTEA and mention me).

I counted how many of these Letters will travel to warmer
climates:

a third of my friends now reside in retirement
communities!

They have lovely names, almost lovely enough to entice
me to move, as well!

Perhaps next year instead of the annual Holiday Letter, I'll
send you a new little

collection of poems, featuring the splendid-sounding

residences where you abide:

Ramsey View, Bay Reef Cove, Jacob's Glen, Oak Green,
The Vine Arbor, Bluff Lake,

Harbor's Wood, and Desert Dusk. Do you blame me?

Here I am, still quietly living alone in a rented apartment
with a church beside me in a

student neighborhood.

I have the stained glass windows next door,

and I can see "my" Saints Windows all night from my
bedroom.

God is in my heart. May He also be in yours.

For I am at peace.

Toujours, toujours, merci mon Dieu, pour cet an si beau.

Fondly,

ANN C. BOW

* * *

Mrs. Peter Evans III
11 Crow's Peak Court
Colorado Springs, CO 80906

Wednesday, Dec. 8

Dear Emily,

A very, very brief note to say that the information in the
Holiday Letter, which I mailed yesterday, is not current!
Almost as soon as I took the Letter to the printer this year,
the children called and said they were planning to come
here for Christmas! They changed their minds, apparently
after Charles insisted that I was getting too old to be alone
for the holidays. Honestly!

I will be delighted to see them, of course, but everyone
getting the Letter will think I'm here alone this year. I
wanted you, in particular, to know, because I sent your
Letter to your son's address in Kansas City, and I know you
won't be leaving for another week. Drop me a note when
you have a moment. I want to hear about your doings. Are
you really able to get around with just a walker these days?
Please be careful on your trip! I wrote Elise the other day,
by the way, but I haven't heard from her for quite awhile.
Do you ever phone her? Has she written? Maybe the letters
from her have been lost. I have heard from my mail carrier

that the new "bar code" put on the bottom of letters and cards is done by computer, and can be wrong! Keep in touch!

Fondly,

Ann

P.S. Do you remember meeting my neighbor, Beth Lambert? Beth fell not long ago, and really cannot stay on here by herself, with these stairs, and all. She has moved to her son's (a nice double-wide mobile home somewhere in Longmont), while they try to find assisted living that takes Medicaid. Have any ideas in your area? I have heard that there is a decent one out in northeast Denver. I guess Beth's apartment will soon be available. It is a one-bedroom, but with no view or underground parking. It has a delightful galley kitchen and charming wallpaper throughout. Some young whipper-snapper professional will probably snap it up! Boulder is starting to fill up with such folks. Perhaps there should be some kind of new folk song, "Where have all the widows gone?"

*　*　*

Mr. and Mrs. Charles C. Bow
10 Arbor Avenue
Bexley, OH 43209

Dec. 8

Dear Charles and Lilla,

How marvelous that you all can come here for Christmas. The accommodations are ready. I think we were very lucky to be able to secure them on such short notice. What would Carson and Adam like for gifts? I can get something for them to use while they are here, if you'd like. I'm sorry I missed your phone call last night ... I was out. And Mrs. Brown left me a message under my door, which I did not see last night. The light in the upper hall, outside my door, has been out for about a week! Until I get my light on inside I can't really see much up here. So, I'm afraid your note got kicked under the tan and red Navaho rug, only to emerge this afternoon when Melodie attacked it!

My Holiday Letters went in the mail yesterday, but I did not have the energy to write a hand-written note on all 83 of them, to tell them that you all would be here, after all. Sometimes the written word lies by accident, doesn't it? By the way, do you think Carson might like to have your father's music stand? She is the only really musical grandchild. Let me know. Will you prefer to dine out, as you did last time, for the Christmas Eve meal? Shall I whip up your favorite holiday dinner, with the roast beef, popovers, and all the trimmings, for our family meal on Christmas Day? I would love to do it, so just let me know. It is no trouble. I was planning such a meal for myself, anyhow! All I ask is that no one tries to DIET during my entertaining. I cook my old-fashioned way for the holidays, even if I do use many new foods day-to-day. (Don't be alarmed, Lilla ... I will not subject the children to too much *nouvelle* [or even *vieille*] *cuisine*!) See you all soon!

Much love,

Mum

P.S. You will finally get to meet Ian Torrence. (But there's no need for you to get him a gift)

* * *

Alicia Bow Montgomerie
324 Parkview Ave. # 12
Jamaica Plain, MA 02130

December 9

Dear Alicia,

I am delighted that you and David can be in town for Christmas. I reconfirmed the reservation for the 3 sets of suites. Is Charles behind the sudden change in plans? I thought everyone had other holiday plans. You two were going to visit friends in New England. I did not truly have much of anything planned, for myself, here. Ian and Wincey may have dropped in, but not for a major meal. Melodie would have entertained me by unraveling the fringe on my throw rugs while we listened to some old Christmas carols. One thing I do miss, from our house, is a fireplace. It would be nice to have one here, especially on a cold, windy Boulder night, with a pot of hot chocolate, a good book, and my fine cat for company.

Thanks for sending me a copy of your design for the natural cosmetics. Your advertisements for the all-natural children's clothing catalogues were stunning (and the children so unusual; wherever do they all live? Enchanting faces.)

I'm reading the new Kate Miller novel, *Home Maker*, and working on a series of brief essays about spiritual insight. Yes, this is your mother speaking, and when you are here I want to take a walk with you and tell you how my thinking has changed (since meeting Ian? Since that Bible Study last fall?) about religious thought and its expression in everyday life. It is never too late to be a reborn Christian.

Love you, dear. Give David a hug from GrammyAnn, and keep one for yourself.

> Much love,
>
> Mum

* * *

The Reverend Thomas L. Blake
The Rectory
St. Luke's Anglican Catholic Church
12 Winslow Lane
Boulder, CO 80302

December 9
Dear Father Blake:

I wanted to thank you personally for the lovely mention of my late husband, Professor Samuel T. Bow, in your sermon last Sunday. Indeed, he was "a charmed man, able to coax music from the very hills and trees of this wondrous place," as you said. It was so thoughtful of you and the Choral Society to perform his "Sonata for Hang Glider and Voices." And it was one of his favorites. I appreciated being invited by the Rawlins to accompany them to the service. I was sorry that you and Mrs. Blake were unable to join us for luncheon at Haye Market.

It was interesting for me to see an Anglo-Catholic service. Dear Sam often visited your church, as you know. I admit that I was raised as a Roman Catholic, and that I drifted from my church quite a long time ago. Sometimes I miss the ceremony, the prayers, and the solemnity. My current church life, at Table Mesa Baptist, suits me well, but gives some pause to the more staid and solemn of my acquaintances. When I say I am "twice born," I get teased about being "twice baked." Ah, Christianity! American churches!

Perhaps you and your wife would join me some winter afternoon for tea over here? My home is small, but the view of the mountains brightens and enlarges it, especially in those quiet hours between four and six. I could show you our modest collection of Bibles. Sam was a King James advocate all his life. I love the King James, but I choose to study from the J.P. Phillips *New Testament*, and the NIV. The spiritual dimension of life, everywhere, is one of my interests. And I have, of course, all of Sam's music here on records, cassettes, and compact disks. Perhaps you would like to hear a piece, or two.

Sincerely,

Ann Cunningham Bow

* * *

December 10

Dear Adam,

GrammyAnn just learned that you and your family are coming to Colorado for Christmas. Do you remember much about your visit here two years ago? You were only 10, of course. I think people really start to have memories that they keep forever, when they are twelve and older. When you were here before, your uncle took you skiing for the first time, and you tackled the beginner's slope in one morning! This time I may stay right here in Boulder when you all ski. It is pretty cold out there for me! I will have some brownies ready for you when you get back here.

Is there anything special you might like to shop for, for your parents while you are here? I thought you and I might go down to the pedestrian mall one day. I would like to spend some time with you. In your last letter to me you mentioned your games. We have a very new store here that has all sorts of computer games and video games. Do you ever play any older games, dear? I have a lovely Parcheesi board, a Backgammon set with ivory playing pieces, several chess sets (your grandfather and I used to play, as did your father when he was a teenager), and some cards. I am pretty good at jelly-bean poker. (I favor the black licorice ones). Have a good flight, Adam.

Much love,

GrammyAnn

P.S. Here are some GrammyAnn Quiz Questions for you:

1. If you were to fly directly south from Detroit, what would be the first foreign country you would encounter?

2. Send me four state capitals from the USA that start with "A," "B," "C," and "D."

* * *

December 10

Dearest Ian,

How are you enjoying that condo at Vail? I have never tried a "time share," although my son and his family have done so on several occasions. Do you have a Christmas tree there? You will approve of my tree! It is decorated now. It's a good thing, too, because I heard just the other day that my children and grandchildren are planning to be in town for the holidays! They'll all be staying over at Flatiron Walk. Have you ever been inside? Quite modern. Two families cancelled, believe it or not, and I was able to secure the rooms we needed.

Perhaps you could come with me next week; I am planning to take a few surprises over, so the rooms will be Christmas cheerful. I have about 12 days in which to get organized ... and there suddenly is so much to do.

Do you much like Santa Lucia coffeecakes? It's one of my traditions to make several at Christmastime. It's the Swede in me. (Just kidding. I'm Dutch-Irish-Scot. In today's "lingo," I might be called a "North-European-American.") I love all things from Scandinavia. These wreath-shaped coffeecakes enchant me. They are fun to bake. I'll make several of them this year, so that you can have one for your sister and brother-in-law over the holidays.

Didn't you say they would be arriving on Thursday, the 16th? I am looking forward to meeting Marjorie, in particular. I do hope she can be coaxed to visit some morning, so we can discuss the Navaho designs in my three oldest rugs. Sam and I found them in the 1950s on a visit, a conference actually, to Tucson. Sam had been commissioned to write a piece for woodwinds and harp to be played at the *Presidio, San Augustin de Tuguison*. He named it, "Prayer for Pima and Peace," as a gesture to the tragedies experienced by the Apaches. When we got back home, he wrote another piece, a work for a string quartet, called "Dragoon Mountains and the Moon."

I'm so pleased that you like Indian art, because I have surrounded myself with a great many weavings and bowls. Somehow having these lovely earth-colored objects near me helps me keep a balance, between my spiritual sense and my everyday self, the one who must dash off momentarily, in fact, to buy bird seed! Tally-ho, dear one. Hope you are enjoying Vail this week.

Cheers,

Annie

P.S. Please have some *Strudel* and a *Kaffee mit Milch* at the Austrian cafe!

* * *

Dec. 10

Dear Cat,

I know I just wrote you and Lilla, but I got something in today's mail that makes me think you had something to do with it ... Did you by chance ask a John Fairleigh to contact me about a retirement community called "Indian Vale" near Colorado Springs? Dear, you know that I am perfectly happy right here where I am, as you will see when you visit over Christmas, and have no plans to give up my independence to live in one of these communities. I actually have a good friend who lives close to it. Many of her Colorado Springs pals have their names on the waiting list, in fact. I am enclosing the cover letter from this man, so you can see how clever and subtle his sales pitch is. I really ought to send the brochure itself to Alicia; with her life in advertising, she would probably be amused to see how these communities try to think of everything an older person might need, then give everything such a sophisticated name that even wheelchair ramps sound elegant! No more brochures, Charles.

Mum

* * *

Mrs. Austin Wills
22 Bent Tree Blvd.
Palm Beach Gardens, FL 33418

Saturday, December 11

Faye Dearest,

I know I will be seeing you in just a matter of days, but I wanted to tell you (in case your brother has been talking to all of you about me and retirement communities) that I really truly do not want to move from this apartment at Dover Terrace. I am terribly settled and comfortable here, can walk down the sidewalk to the Hill for groceries and what-nots, the Post Office, and the University. I am part of this place. Do you know what I mean? So many of my friends of my generation are gone now, no longer living, or moved away. But I am not lonely. I have darling Ian, whom you will meet, but he is in such accord with my nature that he doesn't even see the situation, of my living here alone, as any kind of "problem," the way Charles does. I'm in touch with all my old friends. I may be alone, but I am not isolated. But about the retirement places: I have started getting brochures almost daily; I have a pile here in a basket by my desk. I would like to give them to Alicia when she's here, because of the persuasive advertising jargon!

About your life, dear … don't try to do too much. I worry that you have taken on an awful lot by moving to Austin's home and attempting to fix everything up just the way he wants it. You have already re-papered two big rooms, changed a bedroom into a home office (do bring some photos of that!), started landscaping that huge yard full of tropical trees and shrubs, and decided to let his daughter stay with you both for the coming school semester! When do you rest? Do you ever get to the beach? Is the catering business mostly for fun or income? I don't mean to pry, but I would be willing to help you out, however I can, if you need some help right now. I'm getting a little unexpected new income from a recently published collection of your father's early works for classical guitar. It is not much, but I will share.

I have a few, a very few, activities planned that I hope to be able to do, even though the family will be in town. I'm afraid I'd made the plans some time ago. They are mostly little things, but enjoyable. Perhaps you would like to join me on a few of them, like the excursion with my friend Wincey Kohl to "The Endpapers" in Denver, to look at books. It's an annual event for me, followed by lunch at the Brown Palace. The hotel has been auctioning off lobby furniture. How I would love to have one of the chairs! I have spent many an hour in there, waiting for your father or a friend. Oh, I know I'm rambling, but I know I won't get as much chance to talk to you as I'd like, when you're here!

One last thing—I've been asked to write a brief introduction for a new edition of your father's "Dakono Lullabye and Other Songs," an edition to come out from the University Press next fall. I will show you what I've written when you and Austin are here; remind me! I have more mellow ideas now than I did forty years ago about rural American life. I had a childhood full of drives to tiny towns in the Midwest, places like Girard, Illinois. Dakono, a farming community north of me here, is about as smalltown as it gets. As the years pass, I find that I increasingly enjoy a car ride up past its farms, where the pigs look as big as the buildings! Take care.

Love,

Mum

* * *

Monday, December 13

Dear Carson,

I am so excited about your visit in a few weeks! Your mother and father told me you all could come for the holidays, and I was surprised! I know you will have a good time, because there are so many wonderful dance and theatre events going on at the University, in town, and in Denver. I can get tickets, if you would like, to a ballet. I know "The Nutcracker" will be here, but you might be tired of that. Would you like to see a young dance troupe perform "*Les Patineurs*" ? That has always been one of my very favorites. I last saw it in London, and it was the high point of my winter visit! The "skaters" made it look as if they really were gliding over beautiful ice. I will see about getting tickets, dear. Maybe it is something that the two of us could do together, while your parents and Adam ski. Alicia and David will be with us all, of course, but Alicia was never that interested in dance. She is something of an opera buff. David is really good at all winter sports, and will probably talk someone into taking him up to the big slopes ... Vail, Aspen, Steamboat, etc.!

Another thing you and I could do together is to make cut-out paper and fabric snowflakes, three-dimensional ones made as ornaments. I always give several to the people here at Dover Terrace when I give them their Santa Lucia coffeecakes on Christmas Eve. Do you know how to cut snowflakes from cloth? It takes very sharp, special scissors. It is more fun than it sounds. Making things is always fun, don't you think? I tend to keep a small basket of scraps and odds and ends near my chair, especially when I am watching something on television.

I had better run, to get this in the mail today. I have a few little errands to run downtown. I need some cake flour, currants, brown sugar, almond tea, and cat food for Melodie. And I might take time to pop into my favorite coffee shop for a cup of Kona and a cinnamon bun! Looking so forward to seeing you, dear.

Love and Kisses,

GrammyAnn

P.S. Here is a little poem I wrote when I was in my 20s:

"Dawn"

Dawn flipped the Sun in her skillet,

After chasing the Clouds away;

Then settled down in her rocking chair,

And began embroidering Day.

* * *

Monday morning

Dear Wincey,

I loved our dinner last night. I'd not been to that little restaurant for years. And I acted, this morning, on one of your ideas. I found an answering machine. I dislike being interrupted by calls when I'm writing, whether I'm writing letters or trying to compose a poem. And you were so right, that my time is as precious to me as another woman's jewels might be to her: something to treasure and hoard and protect. Well, I will! And I love being able to stand next to the machine and hear the callers who leave messages. So far today I have received a call from a credit card company, a local charity, my eye doctor's office, and my granddaughter! I poked the button for Carson's call, and broke into the message so I could chat with her. She seemed pleased that I have the machine, and said that her parents have one (a fact I know only too well!)

Carson wanted to know if she could spend one night with me here at my apartment, instead of being at the condominium the whole vacation. Wasn't that wonderful! Wincey, before I forget, I want to invite you for tea with my family on the 23rd, up here. I am planning what to serve. Faye is so particular, and Lilla is such a non-cook, and Alicia is so slap-dash about food that I'm having a bit of a time deciding what will suit everyone. I am going to decorate some more, to make it look like a European *"fête."* I have been rummaging through my bookshelves, closets, and hatboxes of holiday ornaments, looking for some new decorating ideas and for my crystal Christmas balls from Sweden. They look so cheerful in a glass bowl with candlelight. Ambiance: the soft light here at 4, the sounds outside muffled by a wet snow, the scent of black currant tea steeping, Samuel's Christmas music, "Quiet Snow Canyon," and a roomful of loved family and friends. How very lucky I am. Please say you will be able to join us, say, around 4:00. (Forgive my stuffing this note under your door, but I could tell that you were not at home: no light was spilling from your front window onto the loaves of snowy boxwoods beneath your rooms!)

Ann

P.S. In looking through some of my books on fabrics and decor, I discovered in Martin Hardingham's *Catalog of Fabrics* that "wincey" is the name of a linen-cotton fabric whose name comes from a play on the words linen, wool, and kersey. Did you have any idea that you have something in common with a special fabric? Isn't it a fun idea?! Tell me soon how you got your name! Were you given the name in Austria or over here? If you were given the name in Austria, was the "w" pronounced as a "v"? "Vinci." Just to look at it, not to say it, in Latin: "I conquered!"

* * *

Patrick Knighton
Executive Director
LITERACY LIVES ON
23 Coal Canyon Blvd., Suite 11
Boulder, CO 80302   Ann C. Bow
                          Dover Terrace # 10
                          26 Dover Lane
                          Boulder, CO 80302

Tuesday, Dec. 14

Dear Mr. Knighton:

I saw your advertisement in the newspaper, and was pleased to see that your agency needs more volunteers. I hope you won't think that I am too old to do a good job. I learned my own grammar before World War II. I would like to become a literacy volunteer, and look forward to receiving some more information in the mail. I was a tutor many years ago, working through the local YWCA, helping with disadvantaged high school students who needed help with grammar, writing, and reading. I used to meet "my" students at the public library. I recall one day that a young girl, whom I'd not met before our first session, arrived wearing a headset hooked up to a rock music station! And she fully expected to be tutored, in the library, while "listening" to that raucous noise! After that challenge, I was ready for anything. I look forward to hearing from you soon. I will be available any time after January 3rd.

Sincerely,

Ann C. Bow

* * *

December 14

Dear Lilla and Cat,

I'm glad you phoned last night, although that "call waiting" that you have does interrupt the conversation quite a bit. My, but you must be tired after talking with so many people all day!

As I said on the phone, I am more than happy to have Carson spend a night over here, and it will not be an imposition. I am not "too frail" to handle a 14-year-old girl, and I think she and I will have a pleasant time. Charles, I can show her the albums of your photos when you were growing up. And Carson can come with me to do some little errands on the Hill. I will take her over to the university. Wouldn't it be wonderful if she decided to come to school here someday! And if she wants to spend more than one night here, that's fine, too.

Your worry bothered me somewhat, frankly. I wasn't sure if your concerns were for Carson's being a burden to me, or my ability to keep up with her. I am just fine. You both know that. I walk everywhere, am as slim as I was fifty years ago, eat right, sleep well, and think right about myself. I may even be healthier than my own children, come to think of it. I don't have to go to "retreats" and "health clubs" in order to keep my peace of mind.

Charles, I have received yet another brochure about a retirement community. I am beginning to suspect that you have given my name to a central clearing-house, if there is such a thing! Dear son of mine, why!!!??? This one was called Shadow Glen. It is in Florida (I don't want to live in Florida, even if Faye and Austin ARE there!) Its main attraction is that it is built on a coral reef on the ocean, north of Tequesta, and has its own lighthouse. There are a lake, boats, croquet, ballroom dancing, and all kinds of "adult education" courses, offered by teachers from the nearby community colleges. The brochure is very elegant, coral-colored, with thick, glossy pages with scalloped edges. I could take "Jazz Ensemble." I could take sailing lessons. I could "play rummy with the singles on the Starfish Terrace, with a weekly buffet, overlooking the Atlantic." I know that it must sound wonderful to many people, just not to me, not now, not yet. Charles ... NO.

"Hi" to your children, and to Measles, who will have a quiet Christmas at her kennel in Columbus! At least, I hope that is where she will be. It is not really a good idea to try to bring her again. Remember the problem with the apartment rules?

Melodie just attacked a yarn doll ornament, but it is easily repaired. I have so many of them on my tree. Mother showed me how to make them when I was about 8. I'll show Carson how, if she would like. I have an enormous basket of yarn somewhere around here. Lilla, remind me to give you a needlepoint pillow I would like you and Cat to have in your home. It was my first success with penelope canvas. Take care, you two.

Love,

Mum

* * *

Mrs. Maryanne Street
2327 S. Vermont Blvd. #32
Houston, TX 77074

Dec. 15

Dear Maryanne,

I was delighted to hear from you after all this time. I did get your Christmas card last year, but don't remember there being a letter inside. I'm sure I would have remembered it, had it been there, dear, as letters are almost my favorite things. I did receive the photo of you and Jamie, and your sons. And I am so, so sorry to hear that Jamie passed away in October, and regret that I did not know at the time so that I could maybe have been some help to you. Although only a few months have passed since your loss, I know that it must still ache terribly. I hope you have had some family and other good friends nearby to help you through these lonely times. Are your boys and their families fairly nearby? My three are all scattered.

I would love to have you come up here for a visit. It would do us both good! If my guest room had two beds we could be "roomies" again after all this time! Remember how you used to talk and talk into the night without knowing I had dozed off! I sleep less now, so I would be better company. Age has some perks, doesn't it?

Just give me a few days notice and I will have the guest room ready! My family has just changed all their vacation plans; I think they want to "check up on" GrammyAnn, (as the grandchildren call me), and are planning to arrive in Boulder on the 22nd and 23rd. So, I will be tied up with all of them (Alicia was divorced, or did you know that, 10 years ago) until January 2nd or so. After that, all's clear! You asked if I'd heard from Marcy or Danni or Elaine. I hate to admit that I simply lost touch with all of them when they moved from Colorado. I did see Marcy's and Danni's names in last year's Knox College alumni magazine. Did you? But Elaine wasn't mentioned. I hope she is well. I went to our 50th, as you may or may not know. I missed the class photo session, I'm afraid, because I was deep in the rare books collection in the new library and completely forgot about our class photo schedule! So, most people wouldn't have known I were even present.

I do hope you are all right. And I look forward to hearing from you nearer your planned arrival. May your Christmas be a peaceful one. I'm thinking of you.

Fondly,

Ann

* * *

Tuesday, December 28 quite late

Dear, Dear Elise,

I hope your Christmas was a happy one! I still have most of the family here, but that's one reason I'm writing you. A snowstorm prevented Alicia and young David from making their plane from Boston, so they were unable to join us after all! I was so disappointed. Alicia is the one child I have whom I can really talk to. And there are many things to discuss. She and her son have settled for a weekend with friends, after Christmas, somewhere in New Hampshire, so I can't even phone her ....

Cat and Lilla arrived on time with their two. Carson, who is now 14, doesn't weigh as much as her brother Adam, who's just 12. I don't understand it. The last time I saw them she was a lovely young girl. But now she looks like a waif. Her parents never say anything about it. But I have noticed that Carson seems to eat very little. And she is studying ballet, you know.

Well, that's just one issue. The other is that Lilla has become very shrewish, always arguing with the children and with Charles. She tried to argue with me on Christmas Eve, but I would have none of it! I pretended not to hear her. I hummed while I basted the turkey and sliced the cranberry sauce and she eventually moved back into the living room and that was that. But it wore me out!

Up until about noon on the 23rd, not long after they had arrived in town, I had thought we all were going to dine out on Christmas Eve. But the family decided I should do two holiday meals, the 24th and 25th, both in the early evening, as is our family tradition. I actually think, Elise, that it was some kind of test Charles cooked up to see if I could cope with all the details! (Honestly!) I coped! I ordered all the food, for the 24th, by phone from Tonella's Market (old Gerry is still there, by the way) and had it delivered to the apartment by 10 a.m. the 24th. That turkey was in the oven and browning nicely by the time they all phoned me around 3. My biggest problem was simply where to put all the food I had already brought in for the big Christmas meal the next day! I actually "borrowed" Wincey's refrigerator for a day. She thought it all hilarious. But both evening meals went just fine!

Then, on top of everything else, Faye didn't seem very happy. She always sounded chipper on the phone and in her cute notes to me, but in person she seemed worn down and depressed. They flew home on the 26th, because Austin's daughter was coming to live with them, for the upcoming semester at school. I don't think I've told you this (I can never remember anymore what I've put in another letter): her name is Lydia and she is a voluptuous 16-going-on-25-year-old. I think it's causing something of a problem. Lydia suddenly wanted to have an "End of Century" party at their home. She and her mother live in Ft. Lauderdale, and it sounded to me as if December 31st were going to be quite trying! They wanted to fly back well before the end of the month in case there might be some technical problems with airplanes and airports, what with "Y2K."

Elise, you and I have always shared our concerns with each other. I know that you will have something helpful to say! When you have a moment, I would love a note, if only to keep my spirits up. I so wanted this family holiday to be fun. But there are some unusual things going on, and I'm not sure if I'm able to cope right now. When Ian and I are alone to talk, which we have not been able to do since everyone arrived, I think he will be able to help me sort through these situations. Ian is very sensible. He is a thoughtful, dear man. It is pleasant occasionally to have such a compassionate man to lean against in a dim room as we look out onto snow falling on the Flatirons up the way. The family met him briefly, at my tea on the 23rd. Happily for all, he has a hobby that is interesting to most people: photography. He was able to talk to them about equipment, collections, and "capturing the spirit" of people on film, and how some cultures do not permit that. Lilla asked him some fairly blunt questions about his retirement. Cat wore his male version of the Mona Lisa smile, which none of us has ever understood the meaning of. I was kind of relieved when my family went back to their rooms. Thanks for listening.

Much love, as ever,

Annie

* * *

Thursday, Dec. 30 (ALMOST the end of a century!)
Alicia,

Thank you for your calls! We were so sad that the weather kept you both from being here. But it sounds as if your little jaunt up to friends in New Hampshire was a success, and I'm so glad. I know that David had fun there, seeing his friends. I was looking forward, though, to discussing boarding schools with him. You are, of course, surrounded by excellent ones, both public and private, right there. Does he have a preference yet? Is he unhappy with his current school, or hoping to try something new? Or is crime up there something to concern you? As you well know from the news, horrific outbursts can happen at the "nicest" schools. Uniforms certainly make a big difference, in behavior. So does discipline. And I fear that our public schools have very little of either, anymore. The teachers' hands are tied. Everyone is terrified of a lawsuit. The students have the upper hand.

I really cannot believe things have deteriorated so quickly. I never thought I would see such problems in my lifetime.

I don't know what I would do if I had to put you three children through high school today, what with the crime, guns, sex, disease, and general lack of standards. Please tell David I hope he will call me (collect) sometime, so we can talk. He might have had a good time with Adam, if you all had been able to visit. But Adam is still quite young for 12. And he is not very verbal. Of course, forgive me ... but how could anyone be verbal with Lilla present!!!!

When's the last time you saw Carson, by the way? I think there is something wrong, dear. She looks like a skeleton, although she wears baggy clothes and covers up her thinness. She stayed with me for a few days after Christmas, but has moved over to the condominium now. I think she and Adam and their parents are off for skiing tomorrow and will be gone for a few days. Lilla has been something of a handful this trip! She has to control everything. It gets very tiresome. I don't remember her being quite like that. Did you know that Faye and Austin flew back almost right after Christmas? Lydia decided to throw a party for her friends. Poor Faye.

Our weather has been terrific. We drove to The Broadmoor for brunch the other day, and plan to go to Denver for the Natural History Museum and to see a play.

Actually, everything has been nice except for Lilla's moods and Faye's quietness. But I suspect you know more about that than I ever will, my being her mother! Let me know if there's anything I should know, all right, dear?

You remember my good, good college friend, Elise Parker, who moved to an Arizona retirement community in October? I have tried to phone her several times over the holidays (I had sent flowers and they were delivered, so I assumed she was home) but apparently she is on a trip. I bet she took some kind of Christmas cruise in the Caribbean. Lucky thing! Her son lives in California. Nice chap. Will you have any more vacation days after the Christmas break? Or do you have to go right back to work after the New Year? You never know, I might fly to Boston to see you both this winter.

Oh, I don't know what reminded me of this, but there is a professor of music history at a small Colorado college nearby who wants to look at some of your father's unpublished manuscripts. What do you think I should do if he asks to take them away, or have them copied, and so on? I have meant, for years, to ask someone at the University to look through the papers, and now I find I'm unprepared when someone else wants to see them. Several of them would eventually have been published, had your father lived longer; of that I am certain. But I never knew which ones. Perhaps they are not all of the same quality. Some date from long ago. I think this young scholar will expect some sort of fee for adding more manuscripts to your father's published opus. He has briefly mentioned putting the music "on line." I am not sure what he means. I imagine that young David does!

I forgot to thank you for the coffee bean grinder. I have it right next to the cappuccino machine on my counter, and think of you whenever I use either one. I love to use the beans for a change. I need my little rituals, I think. As one gets older, one finds solace and contentment in some of the smallest activities! Thank you, darling. And I will write David to thank him for the books he selected for me. I am looking forward to reading both of them, especially *Rediscovering America*. It looks fascinating. I had always wondered why Baton Rouge and Albany had been chosen as sites for state capitals. Have you read it?

Continue to rest and enjoy the vacation days remaining to you, dear. And know that you are in my prayers and thoughts, as ever. Happy New Year! Happy New Century. Isn't it poignant, or odd, to think that your father will have lived only in this passing century, while we all move on?

Much love,

Mum

P.S. The saddest thing is happening ... a neighbor of mine became ill and has to move into assisted care, but needs one that takes Medicaid. She does not want to leave our neighborhood, yet her sons live in Delaware and Tennessee. The last I heard was that she will move to Tennessee, but still put her name on a waiting list for a new facility in northeast Denver. Even so, that is pretty far away from here, and the poor dear will not be able to come and go. She might be just as well off in another state as to be that far from this neighborhood. She will be limited as to how much money she can legally keep in a bank account if she receives Medicaid at an assisted care home. What a shame that she could not remain here where everything is familiar.

I receive Medicare. Thank goodness for Social Security and the music royalties, small as they are. I try to make wise investments whenever I can. I am lucky. No, I should say I am blessed, really, to be provided for. I do not want to take anything that is not mine to have. There is uncertainty in aging, uncertainty about who will make life-changing decisions about our fate. We old folks sometimes feel like old shoes being shuffled around in a dark closet.

* * *

January 2, the first Sunday of a New Century
Dear Elise,

I have just risen like the phoenix from a tangle of ribbon and wrapping paper I have rolled or folded. The living room is lightly scented with some charming candles in glass containers given me by my granddaughter. The scent is "Spirit," which I recommend as good company when you have time alone and want to feel a presence of some sort; perhaps this is the reason for the phenomenon of burning incense or other fragrant waxes and woods during religious rituals??? The smell itself, as well as the bright flame: means to a mysterious end? Olfactory and visual stimuli that inspire and soothe? I will have to think about this!

Don't mind my ramblings ... I am in such fine spirits today! Part of this is due to having the holidays behind me and part to having my home to myself again. In about an hour I will make my way to church. So uplifting. I love the fellowship. Do people where you are leave for services, or perhaps have some kind of Chapel on the premises? Non-denominationalism at the very end of one's years, after decades of attending a home church ... hmmm ... now that would be an interesting study!

Melodie is on the wide sill watching ... what? The pine boughs are dense with new snow, and the peaks beyond like iced biscotti on a clear blue plate. Listen to me! Is fine food all that suggests itself to me when I want to compare a thing like a rocky mountainside to something exciting? Of course, I did do a great deal of baking and serving these past few weeks, and I have fairly rarified things on my mind, like blue corn meal, demerara sugar cubes, lemon curd, *feta* cheese, *felafels*, and sourdough. And it will take me awhile to "simplify" my cooking again, to cook well just for myself. You know what I mean, Elise. Less white chocolate mousse and more *couscous*! My idea of "simplifying" is to make more work for myself at the market and less work for myself at the stove! I probably am suffering from what Charles teasingly called my "gourmet goggles," meaning that I have an uncanny way of finding cafés, tearooms, gourmet aisles in stores, and elegant sweets wherever I go. Of course, whenever the grandchildren were over, I served something "normal" for them, like a peanut butter and jelly sandwich for Adam and a green salad for Carson. Easy.

I must say, though, that my tri-weekly jaunt, on foot, to the downtown mall for a visit to my favorite café, "The Canyon Creamery," seemed unpopular with Lilla. Why? Was it that Lilla would have preferred one of the pubs (she drinks a great deal of white wine) to my coffee and cake ritual? Part of the problem, of course, was that sitting in a café like that required conversation. Charles preferred to wander around the pipe store with its canisters of moist, rich pipe tobaccos with their exquisite aromas, and the exotic cigar humidor room. I, too, just love to browse through that tobacco shop, and lift the glass lids and take a deep breath. I suspect they didn't much favor my coffee shop because their quiet daughter Carson refused to eat or drink anything in public (I noticed this over their stay) and seemed very ill at ease if I so much as forked a bite of pound cake within her view. Food fads! Oh, my! Does it never end?

All I wanted to do was share some of my favorite habits and routines. I can't wait to hear about your new routines, dear. It must be so interesting to meet new people every day! I do pretty much all I want to, visiting an art exhibit one day, a bakery the next, a bookstore in Denver for a book-signing, a park, my little coffee shop near the river. My days are quite simple. I enjoy little things. I am easily satisfied. My, when did the simple little things that I have strung like antique buttons on a favorite piece of fabric become so boring to my family?

I have more questions to ask about your new life. Some other friends of mine have written over the holidays to exclaim about outings to hear concerts, or to go to a play. They all agree on one thing: the terrific meals provided by the immaculate dining rooms, and the relief at not having to prepare large holiday meals anymore! If you have been on a cruise, I know you have been enjoying fabulous meals!

The kettle is whistling. Melodie yawns at the quiet beyond, scampering across the tan-toned Navaho which wrinkles under her fast feet, and slides towards my tiny kitchen in hopes of tuna. I will sign off now, to have some cranberry tea and crumpets (a gift from Alicia) by my kitchen window, where the iced limbs of the ashberry tap, and fogged melodies faintly treat my ear to organ practice across the way. Choir practice daily: how I look forward to my guessing game of "name that tune," as I strain to hear chords through glass panes and stone walls in the frigid new year air. Please call or write! I trust that your trip was satisfying! *Ciao!*

Cheers,

Annie

P.S. Elise—I'm enclosing two of the prayers I have written, for my newest project; I'm sure I told you about it, but if I did not, let me say, in a nutshell, that it is a little book on spirituality. By the way, I have found a fabulous book— *God is Green. An Ecology for Christians*, by Ian Bradley. I will send you one. It makes marvelous sense.

PSALM ONE

I turn to You, knowing that You know all.

Morning and night

no longer define the day,

nor do they reveal and

conceal
Your light.
A pre-dawn waking
inspires
my prayer. . .
beginning
again
one of my days
within the All
You made:
I praise.

PSALM TWO
Help me, My God,
Early to know
All that I must:
Sacrifice, Trust.

* * *

Monday, Jan. 3
Dear Katya,

What a surprise running into you at the Canyon
Creamery the other day! I had my son Charles and his wife
Lillabet with me. They live in Columbus. Am I correct in
remembering that you grew up in Toledo? I seem to recall
conversations about Lake Erie. But my memory, while still
acute, has recently taken the form of a crazy quilt, and bits
and pieces of the past are stitched together in such odd
shapes that I never know for sure how to retrieve a

particular fact! It's as if I turn the quilt around and around, trying to find a pattern I know is there—like a velvet square between a silk circle and a muslin triangle—and I find the square, but not where I thought it would be.

You asked that I call, but in all frankness, let me say that I am not much good on the phone! Somehow, I find, a phone conversation develops its own path, hurrying up and down and around corners, and taking us on a journey we had not intended. And, more often than not, when I hang up, I find that I have forgotten to discuss the very thing I had originally called to discuss, simply because some comment or interruption changed the track of the conversation so completely that I never found my way back to the fork. So, Katya, here is a small letter, offered as my way of sharing news.

At the moment I am taking a break from packing my holiday decorations. I always pack my wooden *crèche* last. I think I may be superstitious or ultra-sentimental, but I do not like to put the wooden manger scene in tissue paper until all other evidence of Christmas has been packed away for another year. My many Advent calendars and my *crèche* will always be my very favorite holiday possessions, and I hate to put them away.

But in answer to your quick question the other day, No, I am not terribly busy this coming week. It has been a hectic holiday, with lots of family here. But I am ready to rest for awhile. Why don't you come by, say, Wednesday, the 12th, around 4. Plan to have tea. We will chat, and you can stay for dinner. It is no trouble at all. I enjoy entertaining. It is so lovely here in the winter evenings. Shall I expect you, unless you give me a call? See you soon!

Fondly,

Ann

* * *

January 4

Dear Alicia,

We had a blizzard last night. My windows are thick with ice, with some even on the inside, and poor Melodie is in a quandary. She hates the cold and will not sit on the windowsills now because of the ice. But doubting her own instincts, she keeps jumping up onto them, as if to bask in the distant sun. She is driving me slightly crazy.

Did I tell you that I ran into an old acquaintance downtown last week, when Charles and Lilla and I were on the mall, whose husband had once been your father's stockbroker? Her name is Kathleen Gillespie; his was Josh. My, it has been eons since I have even thought of them, but at one time, some thirty years or so ago, we all used to see each other quite often. That was when your father had the sabbatical during which he taught some evening courses at the University of Denver. The Gillespies lived on Evans, very near the college. We used to meet them for dinner. Josh was quite a fan of your father's music. And his wife, whom everyone called "Katya," was a splendid cook who used to make us all laugh with her imitations of various actresses.

When I saw her, very briefly, the other day, it was the first time since your father had died. I know that she knew about it, but whether or not Josh is still living, I do not know. In fact, your father and I had not heard from Josh and Katya for so long that I had actually forgotten about them. But she asked me to call (I wrote a note instead), so we could get together.

You, right now, are about the age I was when we all used to get together. The odd thing, and perhaps the reason I am rambling on about this to you now, is that Katya looked exactly, I mean exactly, the same as she did long ago. It gave me pause. Either I have let time weather me so that I seem much older, or she has kept time from changing her. And that is what intrigues me. Why? Am I the only person I know (with, maybe, the exception of Wincey) who ignores "aging" as a negative change, yet accepts my appearance, while others of my era so dread or fear aging that they go to the extreme of denying change, and seem to peer out of their artificially "youthful" faces with old eyes? Do you know what I mean? I have not colored my hair blond or had a facelift. Yet my mental and spiritual attitudes, in my opinion, are what have kept me youthful. And youthful I feel, believe me. I run rather than walk; I can still wear a Chanel suit I bought abroad when I was 25; and people who meet me for the first time generally guess my age as younger than it is. Yet Katya, with her ash-blond waves, her press-on pink nails, her Gucci "G's" stamped all over her accessories, is an old soul in a toy body. She had a raspy, smoker's laugh.

When she scribbled down her address, I was not at all surprised to see that she lives in a new retirement community near Colorado Springs: The Château du Ciel. It is best known for its golf courses and dining room. I should know! Ask me how many Château du Ciel brochures I have received since last summer, dear! Ah, yes! Your loving brother must have written, called, and faxed them to put me on their list. Funny how Cat would think I would like a place like that! My Goodness! I would move from this delightful home to a deluxe golf course with rooms? I sometimes like to watch a golf tournament on TV, but I have never played, as you well know. Funny how one can raise three children and one of them so entirely and so regularly misses the point about one's character! Now, dear, do not tell Charles Mum is upset with his persistence; I will move someday if I want to move someday. And in the meantime I can spend an afternoon with someone like Katya Gillespie and perhaps learn what it is really like to live in a villa *sans souci*! I think I know.

I trust that you are back at work, although I would love it if you could find another time, even a weekend, to fly out here. I really did miss the two of you at Christmas. Was I correct in hearing Lilla or Faye mention something about your interest in moving? (Note how your mother saved that little question for the end! Ah, I await your response with much anticipation). Of course, I may have totally misunderstood their chatter. And chatter it was! Poor Faye hardly got a word in, what with Lilla's opinions on this and opinions on that. Perhaps they were discussing someone else altogether. I treasure you, dear. Hope to hear from you soon.

Much love,

Mum

* * *

Jan. 5

Dear Cat and Lilla,

We are having a reprieve from real winter today, and I bundled up in my favorite old duffel coat and took a long walk up into Chautauqua. I sat in one of the canvas swings and swung gently back and forth as I watched the town below. Some Oriental students were playing with a beautiful Hungarian Sheepdog. Have you ever seen one? Long, long ringlets of hair. And you cannot possibly tell which end is the front or back! I'm home again, making a pot of Mt. Elbert Blend coffee in my new thermos-style machine, burning an umber-colored candle ("Fry Bread") in a terracotta container, and about to read a Hillerman mystery. I am wearing my new Irish cardigan, a wonderful gift from your dear Adam. Do tell him that GrammyAnn loves to put it on, open the windows, and feel the winter air on her face while she sips coffee and listens to granddaddy's "winterpieces for ice and oboe."

Do you remember meeting Katya Gillespie when you all were here? We had just come out of the café and were about to cross to "Book Ends" to look for the new *Psalms for someone, somewhere,* by Creel Van Eyck, who used to go to my church in Michigan. Anyhow, I dropped Katya a note the other day, asking her to come by next week. Your father and

I used to see the two of them many years ago, back when he had some money to invest after his "Silver Plume Song Cycle" did so very well. [Before I forget, while I am thinking of this: don't worry about how my investments are doing. I have confidence in my own broker. I don't have a very big portfolio, and it is pretty easy to manage. You do not need to give it another thought.] But, as I was saying, as I get older, I generally don't make myself entertain people anymore ... and that is all that is involved when you have someone you barely know over for a few hours. It is not at all the same thing as having a current friend over. I have started to think I might be quite selfish, actually, to prefer my own company, and that of a very few others here, to having a series of brief, obligatory "get-togethers" with former acquaintances. And yet, when I hear from some of my old pals, especially the ones who have moved far away into retirement communities, it seems that their social life consists entirely of a series of brief get-togethers with new acquaintances. And, from what they all tell me, everyone seems happy!

But all of this, to be sure, is not why I am writing today. I wanted to ask if you have, by chance, followed your mum's tiny, well-meaning suggestion to look into the possibility that Carson might be anorexic. She is such a darling girl, but had so little energy when she was here. When we went to The Broadmoor that day, and Adam and you both hurried off to the skating rink and the shops, I strolled about the lounge and eventually sat in my favorite chair near the Maxfield Parrish painting. I spied Carson stretched out on a sofa behind some plants. I don't think she knew I'd seen her. She had a magazine and seemed to be reading, but she looked so pale and worn out. Something about her posture, her having chosen that deserted corner of the lounge, kept me from intruding into her space. Perhaps she was just engaged in romantic, teen-age daydreams. I remember doing that!

Anyhow, dears, do me the favor of making sure she is fine, all right? Perhaps you live so close together on a daily basis that you don't see her as I have seen her. I am quite concerned. You left a message on my phone machine the other evening (I was at my favorite deli, Raleigh's Corner, with a friend) but you spoke so fast I could not make out anything but the word, "business."

By the way, Katya lives at Château du Ciel, one of the many places you have had send me brochures ... I will ask her what it's really like to live in such a spot. If everyone lived as they should in this world, such places might not be necessary. I am referring to compassion, a helping hand, better health insurance and services, adequate transportation for older people, etc. You have heard me on this many times before. And you know that I want to remain where I am. I do not, however, want to be (or to be perceived as being) a burden to my own family. And I am making the appropriate arrangements with my lawyer, so that my *dénoument* will bother as few people as possible.

By the way, before I forget to mention it, I am having "Video Valuables" here in a few weeks to catalogue my things. One of you had asked me to do so, in case I were ever burglarized. But another reason, I realize, is to narrate to whom I want to leave my things, like the Navaho rugs, the pewter, the china, the music equipment, piano, etc. so my heirs won't quarrel.

I will keep in touch! Know that you all are in my prayers, and that I am trying to compose several new psalms for the collection I am working on. I am concentrating on two ideas right now: gratitude and respect for all of creation. Would you like to have them, as I write them? I have an agent, thank goodness, who assures me that the collection will find a publisher. I don't care so much if they make me much money, as that they enrich hearts and souls in this crazy, confused, topsy-turvey world of ours. Take care, dears!

Love to you all,

Mother

P.S. Please cut along my dotted line here and give this page to Adam. It is a little quiz! Ask him if he can solve the questions and then send his GrammyAnn the answers. Tell him that there will be a little reward!

1. Which country is the most northern: The Netherlands, Norway, or Finland?

2. Which of these American river cities have a French name: Baton Rouge, Richmond, Des Moines, St. Louis, Kansas City, New Orleans, Cincinnati? How did they get to have French names?

3. When they were new, in which countries were Hadrian's Wall, The Great Wall of _____, and the Berlin Wall? Were they controversial?

4. Which of these walls was the longest? The oldest? Are they still standing, in part or in whole?

* * *

Sunday

Dear Wincey,

I'm slipping this under your door, because I suspect that you will be back by nightfall. I just had the most disagreeable phone call from my son and his wife. They were both on the phone. He called in response to a letter I'd written, mentioning my concerns about their daughter's thinness. But as soon as he and I started to talk, just now (and he started off quite kindly), Lilla got on the phone, too, and started to shriek that everything that was wrong in their lives was because of me. I heard Charles try to protest, but she overpowered him. The saddest thing was that during a moment of quiet, when she was catching her breath, I heard Carson yelling in the background. A combination yell and scream, as if she were angry and crying at the same time. There was no point in listening to Lilla's outpouring of anger, since nothing I was saying could even be heard above the din. So I hung up!

Now, Wincey, sitting up here alone with my cat, surrounded by family photos, all I can think is that I have failed terribly. I don't think I have been too protective or have interfered with my only son's life. I have given him more independence than he probably deserved. Yet, here he is, a grown man with a family, a successful career, and lovely home in one of the choicest neighborhoods of a state capital, and his family world is full of strain and misery.

It is hard to share the pain a parent knows, isn't it, when a child misunderstands your intentions. I just want Carson to be well. Why on earth should that lovely child be anorexic? And, worse, why should her parents so fear facing the problem, and fear my asking about it? She is my only granddaughter. This whole thing has me terribly upset. I wondered if you could come up later, unless it really is too late? I am going to settle into my sofa and try to study from my book of Psalms. When I'm upset I try to recreate childhood ... like being rolled up in a puff (*eine Steppdecke*) in a room with a nightlight, with my parents in the next room. Soft light, books, pillows, a cotton throw over my knees, a bedjacket, and prayer.

None of the amenities would help in the least, I am sure, if I had not prayer to depend on. And, as you know, for we have discussed it many a time, I don't think of prayer as petition. Prayer, as a child might pray, is petition. Always hoping God will give you just what you want. The prayer from the older soul has little to do with petition. "May thy will be done," ("*Dein Wille geschehe*") comes closer, don't you think? Our sermon this morning (I went to the early service today) was by a visiting minister, from Georgia. He mixed humor and insight into a sermon packed full of astute observations about our society and its demands. And, again and again, in his talk, he weighed the value we tend to place on activity versus the value we place on belief and prayer.

Parents, he said, who are stressed by juggling their children's after-school activities with their own careers and marriages, balancing busyness and greed for the "good life" on the one hand, and a need for personal prayer time on the other, seem to be missing the main message of our reason to be: belief in God, and all that that means. Such a belief is a commitment in itself. A family seeking a better lifestyle, another car, fame for their children in school and athletics, wealth and success, is a family with a hollow core, if God is not at the center. Lilla and Charles do not have God at the center. Maybe that, ultimately, is what saddens me so today. My own son.

Dear, come if you can. I am feeling better already, just for writing this little note to you. I will make myself a cup of sweet tea and some cheese toast and try to focus on grander, greater ideas. Ice is clicking on the window of my bedroom. The alley between me and the church is quiet tonight. The Saints Windows look especially comforting from here. Is there a patron saint of compassion? For misunderstood mothers, misunderstood children? I am a hammer, Wincey, not an anvil. Charles knows that. Lilla has merely spent decades misunderstanding it. Hope to see you later. If it is too late to come up (too late for you, dear, not me ... I expect I will sit here reading into the wee hours), we will talk tomorrow over morning coffee and *brioches* from the Canyon Creamery, *nicht wahr?*

P.S. I had just written my son, asking, among other things, if he or his family might like to see some of my new writings ... and it suddenly dawned on me, that he has never asked to see any of them.

Gute Nacht, Meine Liebe,

Ann

* * *

Monday, Jan. 10

Dear Mrs. Allenby:

I am writing in reply to your advertisement in the Camera for part-time employment as a housekeeper. I liked the way you worded your ad, and I would like to meet you, fairly soon if possible. I twisted my ankle early this morning, in the dark, when I crossed from my bedroom to the hall to get the paper. And I think I will have to stay quiet for a few days. I have some company due, however, very soon, and need some assistance with marketing, cleaning, and caring for my cat, Melodie. My home is a small, two-bedroom, second-floor unit facing south-west at Dover Terrace near the University. There are a cozy kitchen, a bright pantry, one bathroom, and a living room.

Shall we set something up today? You left no phone number, so I am asking a friend to Fax this letter to the paper. The man in Classifieds said that he would be able to reach you by mid-afternoon! The marvels of modern machines! I very much like the idea of reaching you by mail, as I am not much of a telephone person, myself. As you will see as soon as you step foot in here, my life is very much centered on the written word! Too much so, some people might say. If you care to have an interview to discuss times, salary, and your requests, please let me know as soon as possible. If, for instance, you were able to come by today, we could chat over a plate of fresh scones, just brought up by a dear neighbor. Your reference to having been "a lady's maid" years ago in London intrigues me. My late husband and I used to visit London frequently. He wrote music and taught at several universities during his career. I look forward to hearing from you!

Sincerely,

Mrs. Samuel T. Bow

(Ann)

* * *

Dear Elise,

Here I am nearly two weeks into the new year, and I still don't know if you are home yet, or receiving my letters. I do hope, if you just returned, that you will settle yourself comfortably and make a neat stack of the thousands (just jesting!) of letters it seems that I have penned to you lately, and work your way through them as lovingly as if you were strolling through your Arizona garden down there on a fine day.

This has been an odd year, already. The cluster of family was both refreshing and fatiguing. Hindsight blurs some of the joy, actually. At the time, I thought I was thoroughly enjoying the visit. But, now, knowing what I know of the tensions and anger and anxieties, I hardly know if our visit was pleasurable, or not! Carson, my dear, talented little granddaughter, is anorexic. That's an eating disorder, you know, and it means the person hardly eats anything because she thinks she is too fat (even if she isn't!). But they are hesitant to give her problem that name. More on that later.

The other thing is almost too trivial to mention, except that there is a dimension of humor to the episode! Did I tell you that I ran into Katya Gillespie downtown after Christmas? I invited her to drop by. We'd not seen each other in about 20 years, and it seemed appropriate that we try to catch each other up a little, or at least have a cordial afternoon for the sake of old memories and good times. Well! You are the only one I can share this with ... it is too unbelievably humiliating to share with my children, and too odd to share with my other friends.

There I was yesterday, eagerly awaiting her visit, seated in my old stuffed chair by the window, which was lined with my blooming Christmas cacti that day. Melodie was frolicking quietly in a box that had once contained my new juicer. I had been reading, and had several books out on a table. The tea table was pulled over to the window so Katya and I could chat while watching the afternoon shadows decorate the snowy Flatirons. I'd set the table with a linen cloth, a favorite Victorian Chintzware pot for the coffee, and big English cups. The plate holding the tea sandwiches, scones, and Devonshire cream and jam was of another pattern, but just the right size for all the goodies. I thought the table looked quite charming, truth to tell. I had one of Sam's pieces, "Deer Morning," playing and the room smelled ever-so-faintly of fresh bread. I was cheerful, eager to ask Katya about herself, and even prepared to bring forth old memories. You know, though, that I abhor the nostalgic sentimentality that seems to seal one's life up into a dusty old shadow-box, as if Life stopped thirty years ago! I so much prefer to look ahead; but I was fully prepared for an afternoon of only looking back.

So. What happened? The time for her expected arrival came and went. She had phoned, leaving word on my machine that she would, indeed, be able to visit that day. But when almost an hour had passed (and I had put the cream away), I heard a voice calling from somewhere below. I limped over (did I tell you about tripping and spraining my ankle??) and opened the door, and there she was, downstairs. I called out to her, welcoming her up, but she called back that stairs were very hard for her, and didn't my home have an elevator? No, it did not. So I persuaded her to take the stairs, albeit slowly, and make the little trip. (How many steps? About 14). Thus, by the time she reached my door, at the top of the stairs, she was puffing (a smoker, it turned out) and grumpily winded. Not predisposed to be in a cheery mood for tea and cakes, alas.

The whole afternoon was something of a disaster. Childlike as I am, Elise, I had anticipated her "oohing and aaahhing," as most visitors do, upon seeing my home, especially the way the magnificent view is so perfectly framed by the wide window. That day, in fact, it could not have been more stunning: the gleaming sill covered with the jewels of Christmas cacti in their glazed pots, the delicate lace wisps of curtain at either side of the window, and the sky as blue as the enamel of a Danish brooch. The mountainside above the town was ivory. Melodie was trailing some ribbon in a circle; the music was at that moment the trill of flute and French horn against the almost "new age" piano—a delightful scene for all the senses, or so I would have thought.

Katya looked around my living room as if she were scanning a Sale Table at a flea market. How do I describe her look? Disinterested, uninterested, haughty, bored? As if she had scanned a room full of second-hand junk and had found little worth her while. I saw that look. You know, if anyone knows, Elise, that I do not miss much, and I NEVER miss a look. Her look made my heart sink. Obviously, I am too much myself to let her apparent attitude crush me … after all, I know my home is charming! Yet, her look did put a pall on things. As if the lights had dimmed and everything vivid suddenly was plain gray.

"So, this is home now?" Katya asked. Don't even ask about the tone! Remember, however, that when all of us used to wine and dine together way back when, Sam and I lived in a house. I love this apartment ever so much more than I ever loved that house, by the way. But you know that. To me, home is mental … a knowledge of right place, an ambiance expressing beauty and self. Not just a few rooms of antiques or the right pictures, the fashionable plants, fabric "in fashion" *au moment*. My home is in my mind, or should I call it my soul? Psalm 90. "Lord, thou hast been my dwelling place in all generations." In French, Elise, it is even more poignant: "*Seigneur, tu as été pour nous une retraite d'âge en âge.*" A retreat, from age to age.

I like to think that my idea of home is a spiritual one, and that my actual dwelling, by suiting me to perfection, will be seen as perfect by my guests.

Let's sum up the day by simply saying that it got worse. She did not want coffee or tea (just a diet drink, which I did not have). She did not want a tea sandwich or a scone. "How quaint, Ann, you should not have gone to the trouble," was the comment, if I recall. And she complained of her back, her hearing ("Could you please turn the music off so I can hear you better?"), and her marriage. Divorced, three years ago. Josh had not wanted to move to Château du Ciel, apparently, preferring to take an apartment in San Francisco near the club he belongs to up near The Fairmont.

I never got to talk about memories, my life now, or even about my family. Or her family. The whole conversation was one gripe after another, with acerbic comments about my home thrown in as she elaborated about her aches. It was almost funny.

But after she had departed (she stayed through dinnertime but just picked at her plate, and went out into the hall twice for a quick smoke), I became blue. For several hours I sat, surrounded by the party things, feeling ashamed of my lifestyle, my little home, my (deliberately) mismatched china, even my husband's music. Her visit had the effect of an evil pall ... how else can I put it? Her visit was like the visit of the bad witch in Snow White: my apple was poisoned. My apple! Listen to me! I treasure my home, my music, my books, my lifestyle, my choice to have pared down my life, to live simply with a few treasured things, with a view that uplifts and friends that understand. And that is exactly where I erred: I had tried to link up my world, me, with someone so different from me that the attempt not only killed the relationship, such as it was, but also tarnished me.

I have so many things to do: train a housekeeper, contend with Lilla and Charles about Carson, meet with Common Prayer on projects, prepare for a poetry reading, meet with a music professor about Sam's work, and on and on and on. My life is full: full and beautiful, like a vase bursting with vivid flowers, like a table piled with delicious foods, like a night sky thickly encrusted with brilliant stars, like a soul overflowing with prayer. I should know better than to introduce anything erroneous.

Katya's visit taught me a valuable lesson. (I am not too old to learn, Elise.) I do not need this. I know so well who I am that I should not need to bring people back from the past; there are, actually, no "good old days" if the people from those days are not good anymore. I live right now, this very minute. I have you, my children, my books, my psalms, my church, my husband's music, my view, my coffee beans and scented candles, my funny cat, my collection of cups, my hopes, my prayers. I do not need to delve in the past for buried treasure, Elise. There is no treasure there. Remember J. Frank Dobie's wonderful book, *Apache Gold and Yaqui Silver*, about the lost riches of the Indian desert lands? Let the legend live. If there is treasure, let it lie untouched. The old memories, dredged up by someone as bitter as Katya, became dross.

Elise, I am beginning to worry that you and I are starting to drift apart, because I've not heard from you in so long! Please, do not become the kind of friend who gradually dissolves like sugar in a cup of tea, and vanishes in the depths! Distance: space, a few mountain ranges, and a state line do not have to separate us. We are only as far apart as we let ourselves be. Be real for me! I might be just a little paranoid because of the Katya incident!! Do reassure me! I need your replies; otherwise, all my epistles are but missiles sent into outer space, orbiting the past. How about a nice, fat, fat, fat letter from you?? Make it long enough to require me to design an entire day around reading it! Make it a two-*brioche*, one pot of Kona, three-candles kind of letter. You are the one I tell all. Do you remember when Gertrude Stein played around with the visual impact of letters in a word? Look at the height, the pride, the glory, of my word forest here: "I tell all." I think Miss Stein would have looked at

that sentence and approved its strength, simply on the basis
of the height of the letters. Cheers!

ANNIE
```
        T
  E L I S E
        L
      A L L
      N
      N
```

* * *

Jan. 14

Patrick Knighton
Executive Director, LICENSE FOR LITERACY
23 Coal Canyon Blvd., Suite 11
Boulder, CO 80302

Dear Mr. Knighton:

Thank you for your letter of January 10th, with some
specific volunteer opportunities at LICENSE FOR LIT-
ERACY. [When did you change your agency name?] I was
daunted, at first, by the application form, but I have filled it
out, and am enclosing it herewith. And, per instructions, I
will begin by saying why I am interested in becoming a literacy tutor.

I have had no formal teaching experience, but I used to
volunteer as a parent at my three children's various schools
years ago. I am a published poet, and am involved with
readings and special events at our public library. I also read
some Latin, French, and German, but (alas?) do not have
Spanish. Is that truly a problem for the kind of position I
hope to have as a volunteer? I enjoy working with people of
all ages, and am ready to begin soon.

Frankly, one reason I'd like to help people learn to read, is to help them learn to speak clearly, as well. The old "standard English" of my lifetime is rarely heard anymore, since so many young people learn their language—grammar and phonetics—from radio and television people, many of whom speak incorrectly. ("Between he and I," for a frequently-heard example!) This has become one of my hobbyhorses! My own grandson in the Boston area has picked up speech habits from the variety of children (and their teachers and coaches) he associates with in his public school; he is as likely to slip into sub-standard English as not, and it apparently is not corrected anymore at school, because teachers have been convinced (wrongly, I think) to assure that each ethnic and cultural sub-group in the nation should be encouraged to express itself in its own speech in any situation.

In all countries, there is a "standard" spoken and written language, and often many dialects of a regional or ethnic nature, often not understandable even to other speakers of the various other dialects. The Viennese dialect is quite different, for instance, from High German, the "standard." An educated Viennese speaker would use the standard language when writing, for instance. In the United States, unfortunately, one is now labeled "politically incorrect," if one comments on the disturbing trend of the increasing dominance of non-standard English. I firmly believe that clarity and accuracy of speech, and of the written language, enable one better to grasp and use abstract language, to increase one's vocabulary, and, in general, to use one's mind. A limited vocabulary of monosyllabic slang will not take anyone very far in any vocation. A nation needs to be held together by a national language. Look what happens to politics, to peace and prosperity, when a national language is not required anymore, and hundreds of local languages or dialects, suddenly spring back up, region by region, in places like the former Soviet Union, the Balkans, Los Angeles! Each of those national languages is important and of value, just not necessarily to a new citizen here who should be required to learn English. That is my opinion.

I wanted to enquire whether or not it is permissible to have the student come to my home. I live on the Hill, only minutes from the campus, and a brief walk from the nearest city bus stop. I eagerly await news about my formal application.

Sincerely,

Ann C. Bow

* * *

APPLICATION—Form 1257-A: Volunteer, Class B

DIRECTIONS: Fill out in triplicate. Keep blue copy. Return white copy. We are an Affirmative Action agency. We do not discriminate on the basis of national origin, race, religion, gender, health, age, education, marital status, or disability. Hispanic speakers and women are encouraged to apply.

NAME	LAST	FIRST	MIDDLE
SELF	Bow	Ann	Cunningham
SPOUSE/OTHER	Bow	Samuel	Tremayne

DATE OF BIRTH	YEAR	MONTH	DAY
SELF	1926	March	19
SPOUSE/OTHER	1915	October	12 [d. 1991]

MARITAL STATUS: M___   D___   S____   W __
CoHabit___ (? Is "W" widowed? X)

OCCUPATION:_Writer, Homemaker

SPOUSE/OTHER: Professor of Music, composer, critic

REFERENCES: Elise Parker, Ramsey View, Unit 6R, Monte Vista, AZ 85324

ADDRESS: Dover Terrace #10, 26 Dover Lane, Boulder 80302

OWN:___ RENT:_X_ OTHER:___ HOW LONG? 9 years

INTERESTS: Music, poetry, literature, travel, Indian art, Christianity

EDUCATION: B.A. 1947, Knox College; M.A. 1948, Univ. of Michigan

PERSON TO CONTACT IN CASE OF EMERGENCY: Mr. Ian Torrence, 757-3186

BEST TIMES FOR TUTORING: anytime after 10 a.m. Mon-Fri

IF YOU ARE ACCEPTED, YOU WILL HAVE TO SHOW THAT YOU HAVE INSURANCE AND A DRIVER'S LICENSE. YOU WILL SUBMIT TO A BACKGROUND CHECK FOR PROOF OF NO PRIOR CRIMINAL RECORD. YOU WILL SIGN A FORM ALLOWING OUR STAFF AND CLIENTS TO SEE THE RESULTS OF YOUR HIV TESTS IF ANY OF YOUR BLOOD SHOULD GET ON THEM AT ANY TIME FOR ANY REASON. IF YOU INJURE A CLIENT WE WILL NOT BE HELD RESPONSIBLE FOR REPRESENTING YOU IN A COURT OF LAW. WE RESERVE THE RIGHT TO TERMINATE THIS VOLUNTEER CONTRACT AT ANY TIME. IT IS ADVISED THAT YOU CARRY A MAJOR PERSONAL LIABILITY INSURANCE POLICY. THIS FORM IS TO BE NOTARIZED AND SENT BY CERTIFIED, RETURN RECEIPT, POSTAL SERVICE DELIVERY TO THE FOLLOWING ADDRESS: 1100 EAST PARKWAY, SUITE 34, NEW YORK, NY 10155.

* * *

January 14

Dear Faye,

I thought this would be a good time to write you a quick note, as I am about to go over to the mailbox to send my formal application (!) to LICENSE FOR LITERACY, where I hope (I think ...) to become a tutor of English to new immigrants, local native English speakers who cannot read, and "at risk" teens. But, frankly, after filling out their form, I'm not quite as enthusiastic!

It is raining today, quite rare here this time of the year. It has washed the snow off the ground. Everything outside is swirled together like Halvah, one of my favorite sweets. I get it at the new candy store on the mall. That reminds me, I have truly enjoyed the basket of treats you sent me for the New Year! Let me thank you again! What a clever idea. I put the streamers and little foil party hats on my table for New Year's. Last night I had Wincey and Ian up for a glass of sherry and we laughed at the fortunes in the cookies you'd sent. One of mine said, "No deed goes unnoticed; no good deed goes unpunished." Melodie, in particular, loved the serpentine, which I had draped from the wall sconces to the curtain rod and across to the stereo antenna! She became completely wrapped-up in the bright pink.

I had not seen Ian for awhile. After the holidays he went west to stay with his son in Carmel. We missed each other. He is such good company. When he and Wincey and I get together we just laugh and laugh. I have not had a chance to tell you anything much about Ian, dear. He has had a full life, is a widower with one son, and is wonderful company! Ian was an executive in an international copper company, based in Phoenix and Milwaukee. He grew up in Wisconsin, is a photographer by hobby, and something of an expert on Edward Steichen. I have learned a great deal about art photography lately! You have heard of Alfred Stieglitz, the photographer and husband of Georgia O'Keeffe. Steichen and Stieglitz were partners and friends. Steichen was the son of immigrants from Luxembourg who moved to the copper mining area of the Upper Peninsula in 1881, I think he said, (I remember the date because that was the year my father was born) so their little boy could have a life in America. Steichen was apprenticed to the American Fine Art Company in Milwaukee, then took his work to the Art Students' League in Chicago (my own favorite American city, as you know!). In 1900 he passed through New York City and met Stieglitz, on his way to Paris. And five years later they opened their very famous 291 Gallery in NYC, that introduced our country to painters like Matisse, Cezanne, Picasso. And Wincey, being Viennese, is familiar with the "Secession Movement" in Vienna, as well. We have such fun, Faye, with my art books, Ian's signed prints, Wincey's anecdotes about the art life in Europe. These are the most fun times for me, being with friends who know something about art and photography, European cities and culture. Ian and his family often dined at The Pump Room, as did my family and I, at Chicago's Ambassador East Hotel! And he and his late wife, Millie, always stayed at The Drake, as did your dad and I! Small world, small world. They don't make many hotels like those anymore, either.

You may or may not remember that your maternal grandmother was born in Wisconsin. She, too, went to Chicago as a young person, to make her way in the art world, but piano in her case. That is where she met my father. And your own father's music degree is from Northwestern, 1936. How I wish you three children could have become more familiar with Chicago!

I put your father's "Open Air Opera" on, in its new CD from Chinook, and Ian was fascinated with the way your father had mingled the tenor and counter tenor in that passage with the woodwinds and water. Do you remember that? Do you remember our all going to Royal Gorge, hoping to tape falling water or the river? And you, who were still so very young, refused to walk to the bridge, because you said you could not see any bridge or water. We carried you over, and there the river was, thousands of feet below! Oh, those were fun times.

I have a housekeeper now: Ellen Allenby, a former lady's maid in London, will be coming once or twice a week to do some light housecleaning for me. The other day, she and I sat over a pot of tea and talked. She talks a blue streak once she starts! I'll have Wincey up to meet her, and they will get along tremendously! I can just see it: Ellen whooshing along with a feather duster and talking about how England has changed, Melodie chasing her and leaping at the feathers, and Wincey sitting by the window doing needlepoint. It will be a colorful scene.

I think I'm doing a reading at the library this spring. I had to cancel one just before the holidays. I usually enjoy such things, as it gives me a chance to see people I rarely see anymore. And it is so lovely to be above the creek in that modern room in the children's library wing. Remember when you and I used to go there for story-hour on weekends? When you were seventeen you helped put on a little art show with my Scout troop, remember that? And I had to miss it all because Carson was born that week in Columbus! Now Carson is almost 15! But I don't feel as if I have aged at all, just that all of you are all grown up!

You didn't mention Lydia the other day when you phoned. Is she in a public school? Or is she attending that pretty Benjamin School nearby? Do you have to drive her everywhere? I admire you for taking on a teenage step-daughter! But take care of yourself, too, dear. You work hard, and I worry sometimes that you think too much of everyone else. And how is the landscaping coming along? Did you select the plants for your patio? If you take any photos, please send me some.

Don't ask me right now how I'm faring with Lilla ... she is very upset with my worry about Carson's health. But if you talk to Charles, go ahead and say we have discussed the situation, and that I send my love, as ever, to them all. I will write again soon!

Much love,

Mum

P.S. I almost forgot to answer one of your questions ... actually, I do not think it is a good idea to have Austin's Mother move in with you, even if the house has enough room. If her income level will not permit a private room in an assisted care facility, but she does not qualify for Medicaid, and she cannot bear the semi-private room where she is now at the place in West Palm Beach, then I think you should ask Austin to ask his brothers and sisters to help him rent her a one-floor apartment near one of the family and help pay for a part-time nurse. I thank God daily, dear, that I have not had to face that particular set of circumstances.

* * *

Monday, January 17th

Dear Ian,

Thank you, dear heart, for coming by the other night. It is harder and harder for me to share you with your family. I know that your son and his wife need you in California for their daughter's surgery, and I know you will be a great blessing to them all. I am just being selfish. Please forgive me! I have treasured your little notes and gifts this past month. I have the Horowitz celebration of Mozart on right now, in fact. And I picked up Edward Steichen's *A Life in Photography*, and find it most entertaining. Thinking of photography: we do not have a photo of each other.

I'm fine. My ankle is not bothering me much. I wanted to assure you that I am up to our engagement Saturday to go to the Springs. As I said the other day, what fatigues me more than anything else in life right now is my having to explain again and again and again, to my son and his wife, that I am fully capable of living here in my little apartment alone. My new housekeeper, in answering the phone, told Charles that I'd sprained my ankle recently. When she left, she put the machine on, as I was downtown making copies of my poem, "My Company" (which I enclose for you), and meeting someone for coffee. So, when I got home, there was Cat booming out of the recorder, demanding (!) to know how I'd fallen, what I thought I was doing living alone at my age (!!!) and causing HIM so much worry. Imagine! Ian, really, sometimes I would like to trade him in on a pet. Does your son act this way towards you? Or are "older gentlemen" permitted an independence not granted "older ladies"? It made me so furious that I put on my walking pants and down jacket and my new knitted hat and stomped right up 13th Street and did not stop walking until I reached the swing at Chautauqua. And, wouldn't you know it … as I was marching along, didn't Katie Mullins step out of her house up on Baseline and try to wave me in, determined to quiz me about you, I am sure! I know she saw us last week at the film at the library. And she is SUCH a gossip. I know, because she always attends my poetry readings, and can't wait to deluge me with questions about my friends. Oh, me. I am rambling … but I did want to get a note to you, because I was feeling kind of sorry for myself today, and thinking about you does cheer me so!

If you were here right now, I'd offer you some hot chocolate and one of the cranberry muffins I just took out of the oven. I'm seated in the kitchen, in fact, and am about to give it a complete cleaning, as I have been baking all day, and have clouds of flour, hills of fallen barley, trails of dry oatmeal, and even a few splashes of crushed berries on the floor. It is quite decorative. If it were an oil painting or a photograph, I could submit it to a local art gallery for display, and call it something like: Prelude to a muffin.

Love you— Ann

MY COMPANY

Without calling ahead to ask
if I may visit,
I visit myself.
It is never known
ahead of time
what I will find:

order, disorder, joy,
spring cleaning,
or coma.

I answer the ring.
From a dark doorsill
I step into warmth,
to see myself
the way I see
me
when no one stands about to chide me for choosing
my own company.

Words and spice tea and bread rising,
an ecology of conscience and spirit,
children and pleasure and silence,
rest is possible. God is like me.
When I'm outside waiting
to enter,
when there is
time,
time permits this. Inside/outside ... a visit insists.

The curious fact remains that other people do not
visit
themselves,
or often. Instead, lazily, they ask everyone else,
"Hey, you, who am I?"
I glance around,
pleased that I am content today,
trusting, and waving
for me, my guest, to come closer.
I am in my dwelling place for all
generations.

* * *

Tuesday, January 18

Dear Carson,

Thank you for having a copy of your ballet program sent to me. It came today. I was delighted to see that you were the lead dancer in a ballet made famous by the Tallchief sisters years ago. And your Bexley troupe, The Capitol Ballet, certainly seems to have a varied and exciting *répertoire*! Congratulations, honey, on being such a vital part of the troupe. The photo of you, with your choreographer Denis Chatton, is very lovely, and flattering. You are photogenic, but don't try to become any thinner now, do you promise?! I don't want you to disappear!

I have been saddened that you have had to hear your parents and me quarrel on the phone (how I HATE the phone!), about what we each think is best for you. I got their permission to write you about how I feel about all of this, honey. We all love you so very much. I do hope it will be possible for you to choose someone to talk to, if you so wish. You daddy told me that you have asked to leave school for awhile. Do let me know what you decide, as I am always interested. And if you would like to come out here and stay with me, that would be terrific. I would be happy to take you to the arts programs around here and Denver.

I was uncertain about things, too, at your age. I was living in Illinois and a student at a large parochial school. Everything was very orderly, and we had lots of work to take home each evening. I had some friends, but I never felt as if I really belonged to any particular group of friends. I was a teenager at the beginning of WWII. My uncle was killed in France in 1944. Everything was hectic and anxious. I found it hard to enjoy parties. The older boys from our town were all in the service.

Many years after my schooldays were past, I summoned up the courage to ask my father why he had seemed so uninterested in my education. He was so startled that I asked! He looked at me and smiled and said that he had not wanted to interfere with my schooling, so he had kept quiet and let me make most of the decisions. That was certainly the truth! But I had never looked at it that way before. Indeed, I was the first woman in my family ever to graduate from college or go on to graduate school. I was so glad he and I had that little talk, because, otherwise, I might have gone through my life (and I am nearly 75!) misunderstanding his attitude. And I don't want you to make the same mistake, dear. What you think you see and hear might not be quite what the other people are really trying to say to you. You may hear pressure and ambition and impatience, when what is being said is really being said with excitement, pride, and love. Everyone wants you to be happy, Carson. Know that, as you make your choices. You have talent. And you have supporters, dear. Do take care of yourself. Keep an eye out for a small surprise from "High Tea," (with a promise from your Aunt Faye that nothing was fattening!)

Love and hugs,

GrammyAnn

* * *

Jan. 18

Dear Charles and Lilla,

I wrote Carson a brief letter, telling her she is welcome here. I am mailing both letters momentarily, so I do hope they arrive at the same time. I laud your effort to get her to meet with someone who might talk with her, and I realize that you hold me responsible for this decision in the first place. I read about anorexia in some magazine last year, and it can be cured. The clinic you mentioned on the phone last night sounds like just the ticket, doesn't it? What was its name? Pathway House? Imagine there being centers for eating disorders!

From what I have seen of Columbus in my many visits there over the years, that city has just about everything a city could have! I am just crazy about German Village, the shops and restaurants, and the art museum. Do, please, let me know if Carson opts for treatment of some kind at this special clinic. And, also, let me know how Adam is taking all this. I hope he is not frightened. Thank you both for trying to see my side in this issue, and for realizing that I am not trying to cause trouble, but to help avert it. The two of you have been so close to this whole situation that you simply have not seen it, the way someone from afar can. Let's all pray for success. And let me share a line from Deuteronomy 33:27 that I found early this morning when I was reading,

"The eternal God is thy refuge, and
underneath are the everlasting arms."

Carson is not alone, dear ones. None of us is.

Love and hope,

Mother

* * *

Wednesday, January 19

Dear Elise,

What a day! I should be in Arizona. We had a blizzard last night. There was an avalanche right out here on the Flatirons, but no one was hurt, apparently. I can barely see the street this morning. Usually, as you know, we have blue sky all winter. But this is something else. I feel very cozy in here. I had planned to have some people up for an afternoon of music and talk, but I've already had one call that someone can't make it. I don't blame her. She lives in a house near the top of a street in the north part of town, and those roads are murder. I had also hoped to go to church tonight, for the

"Winter Dinner" and hear a visiting minister from Houston talk about "Merged Families in the Eyes of God." But I will have to skip it now.

I am in charge of a Valentine Affair at the library next month; it is a fundraiser for the local home for battered women and children. I have spent a lot of odd bits and pieces of time for the past few months getting things lined up. I am actually looking forward to the challenge of creating a mini-festival of music, art, foods, and readings that will attract enough people for our group (this is the church group, Common Prayer, that I joined) to raise the hoped-for $5000 to renovate the bedrooms at the shelter. My church is one of about seven in the area who help with community projects of this kind. If you were here (can you come for a visit next month and lend us a hand?!) I would put you to work designing the displays. Your knack for color and captions would certainly help. I have someone to design the posters and to contact the media. I hate doing that myself. I know I should delegate more of these activities to other people ... but I still think if I want something done right I should do it myself. Not much of a team person, am I? Ian was going to do some photography for the marketing but he will probably be out of town too often between now and then to be able to.

I tried to call you last night, but the line was busy for so long that I am taking it upon myself to ask that you get call-waiting! I don't have it, to be sure. But Charles and Lilla do (I have been "bumped" so often that I have stopped phoning them). They swear by it. Elise, I was pleased that you are home again. Do call or write! I'm beginning to feel out of favor! Did you like the basket of tea loaves and the berry vinegars? I had Faye select some for you. "High Tea" is doing fine. Faye sells to a clientele down there which I might call *nouveau riche*, but which the press refers to as "new millionaires," apparently investors who held the right stocks at the right time! Some of these households are so palatial in their décor and lifestyle that they actually hire someone called a "House Manager" to do ALL the jobs and chores that used to be done by a domestic staff, or, in a smaller home, by the wife. Of course, in south Florida, Faye says domestic help is all Hispanic, or Haitian, from the islands. Since virtually no one, except affluent Cuban or Colombian families down there, who needs domestic help can speak Spanish, or French, most people are really up the creek! And, would you believe, there is a training center for these new managers here in Denver! They "do" parties, silver, plumbing, invitations, linens, care for antiques, deal with the grounds! My!!

I've been working on a new series of psalms, and have especially enjoyed rising a little earlier every day, so I can really study the words used again and again in Psalm 34. Just think about this image: "The angel of the Lord encampeth round about them that fear him, and delivereth them." "Encampeth." I love it! I want to use it myself in a poem. Think of me here with Melodie (and sometimes with Ian, dear man), sipping mulled cider, watching the snow, and reading ancient words. I am happy.

Annie

* * *

January 20

Dear Katya,

Your note came in today's mail. I'm terribly afraid that I won't be able to do much of anything for awhile, because of my ankle. I stay home mostly. Isn't it nice for you that you have your bridge group at the club during these snowy days. Some of my friends play bridge, but I have never had the gift. Most games are hard for me. But I manage to keep busy rattling around my tiny home. Enjoy the winter!

Best,

Ann

P.S. No, you did not leave your scarf here. I looked for a blue and gold Hermès print, leaves and vines, as you said, but it is not here. I found a pack of your cigarettes under the chair, but I am afraid I threw them out!

* * *

Professor Thomas P. Jenkins
Department of Music
Glenmoore Community College
Glenmoore, CO 80305-2478

January 20

Dear Dr. Jenkins,

Your letter was waiting for me when I returned from a visit to the library. I had ridden the bus downtown. I found a little festival taking place in the corridor over the creek. You know our city library, don't you? There was a book-signing in the main room, children's story hour in the big room, and a demonstration of a computer system in the annex. It was all quite exhilarating, and made me feel part of modern culture. My late husband would have hurried home to compose a piece to reflect the mood. He probably would have called it "Library for hush and horn," or something! How much fun we used to have naming his music!

I am free for lunch next Thursday, the 27th, if that continues to be convenient for you. Shall we meet on the mall, perhaps around 11:30, and then come up here to look at some boxes of papers? Perhaps you won't have to take that many away with you. There is a copy place down the street where you could have some papers copied, if that would work for you. Let's meet at "Librettos." It features delicious *tapas* and *flan*, and always has opera playing. The décor might interest you—historical posters from Central City's old Opera House. The great Melba, who sang there, is featured as the motif, if you will! A music lover's place, to be sure.

Perhaps we will be inspired as we attempt a search of dear Sam's music. I will be interested to see what it is you are hoping to find. I have not gone through the boxes for a number of years. There were some works in progress. I hope you know about copyright laws.

Sincerely,

Ann C. Bow

* * *

January 21

Mrs. Peter Evans III
11 Crow's Peak Court
Colorado Springs, CO 80906

Dear Emily,

What a letter! Your vacation to Kansas City must have been the high point of the year, for sure! Imagine your mother insisting on reading the Nativity Story to her great-great grandchildren! How wonderful! From your descriptions of your son's new home in Shawnee Mission, Santa himself must have thought he'd gone to Heaven! What a place to spend time! And to be able to spend a month with your son, his wife, their two children, and your three great-grandchildren ... aren't you simply exhausted????

I just loved your packet with the snippets of wallpaper samples and carpet samples from the house. They have taste. The hues are my own—colors of the southwest. But isn't it interesting how colors today are named? In our day, don't you know, we had red, pink, blue, brown, green, and so on, while today's decorators name colors thematically or according to some dimension of the natural or political world. Where we had "white" they have "Navaho White," or "Melon," or "Starlight." Where we had "coral," they have "Bimini Dawn," or "Pottery." I love it!

After I looked at the lovely little squares of carpet and the stack of wallpaper samples, I actually walked around my own little home and "named" all the colors of all the things I own, as if a real decorator were giving a demo: "Colors of A Widow's Den." How does that sound! And here's what I found (my new names, of course): Mesa Beige, Sandstone White, Treeline Green, Forest Floor Grey, Tree Bark Brown, Snowstorm White, Chinook Sky (a dappled look), Dry Creekbed Tan, Burnt Conifer, Biscuit, New Cream, Bonechina Blue, Cranebill Gold, and Sleepless Black.

Naming things keeps me from being too possessive, too greedy. As soon as something unnamed is named it has an identity in the seer's eye, making it possible, I think, for the seer to release it. If I had to walk away right now from everything owned, and named, in my home here, I could do it. For the things I truly love and hold dear have names independent of their presence, or absence: God, my Samuel's music, his love, my love for him and our children. I am a lucky woman, Em, to be part of something rich and enriching, and free of place and things at the same time. What we call home has so much more to do with imagination than with objects. So much more to do with being at peace than with ownership. Your assemblage in Kansas City, your multi-tiered family of five generations, is as rich as anything in life can be: a big, layered, delicious chocolate cake of a family! But isn't it good to know that the riches we have, in our family, love, and talents, surpass all beauty of thing, all nomenclature, all "objectification," and simply exist?

Your moving account of Christmas Eve—the traditions, the lace and linen, the old dolls dressed for a party, the music, the fun—contrasts tremendously with my own experience this year, where, unfortunately, tension tried to overcome compassion. I did my best. But my relief when everyone went home made me realize that the gathering had not been as special, if you will, as I had hoped it would be. I love my children, and theirs. I was relieved to see them leave. Troubles will pass. And we made new memories.

You have a real gift, with your ability to collect and assemble actual mementoes of an occasion, like these delicate squares of paper and fabric, of reproducing the mood of a place and a time. Your Christmas in that sumptuous setting is now as real to my senses as my own experience here. Thank you for that!

I have to mention that fabulous catalogue from the Nelson-Atkins Museum! I have been reading it, and, so far, my very favorite paintings are Monet's wintry *"Boulevard des Capucines,"* and the breathtaking "Olive Orchard" by van Gogh. In both, so very different paintings, I get a strong feeling of the dominance of change and power in Nature. And the expression on the face of El Greco's "The Penitent Magdalene"!! I am savoring this book, and have decided to visit the museum myself when I can do so. Perhaps my friend Ian Torrence could accompany me. He would love the collection.

And thank you, too, for my other lovely present. I can never have enough editions of Emily Dickinson! This one is so pocket-sized that I have already put it in a pocket ... I really have! And it will ferry with me as I walk up and down the Hill, exploring my ever-new neighborhood, and my thoughts. There is NO ONE like that Emily to hold a sure candle to the soul, and to reveal the ideas. You are a great pal, Em. And I look forward to our day together this spring! One thing we can discuss is this whole "problem" our grown children seem to have with our living "independently" in our own homes. If we were ill or disabled, I would be the first to take appropriate action so that I could be properly cared for, but not in one of THEIR homes. I don't plan to be a burden. I understand completely how your son wants you to move to the KC area, since Charles has similar plans for me. But I am resisting his plans, even though I must receive several retirement community brochures each week in the mail. What an industry that has become ... moving settled people into new settlements. Put that way, it almost sounds Biblical! I know these communities are suitable, even desirable, for many older people. I just do not care to make such a big move, quite yet. On that note, I will leave you, and start making preparations for dinner!

Much love,

Annie

* * *

January 21

Mr. Karl M. Williamson
56 Peak Place, Suite 202
Boulder, CO 80302

Dear Karl,

I have not been in for several months, as you know, but I have been following some of the ups and downs of this interesting market on CNBC. I wanted to come by some-time, perhaps take you to lunch downtown, and discuss my investments in general. When my son was here recently, with his family, he asked me if I had "protected" my estate with some annuities and insurance. I told him I had every-thing in order. I did not care to go into detail in front of the family, of course. But as I read over my last account state-ment, I noticed that one of my mutual funds has done very well. I will probably use some of that fund to make some small gifts this year. I have been so busy with the holidays and some upcoming projects that I feel I have neglected my business affairs. Let me know what would be a good day for us to meet and talk.

Sincerely,

Ann Bow

* * *

Jan. 22

Dear Alicia,

I have Copland's "Quiet City" on the CD player. I am snowed in—not actually snowed in, dear, but mentally snowed in! I want to be home by myself today.

The students who live across the street in the three-story brick house with the row of pines in front have worked all morning to make a winding row of snowmen. Each is quite different from the other, and all are garbed in bright scarves. When I was out much earlier, to knock snow off the bushes by our sidewalk, I was invited in for a cup of real hot chocolate by Wincey. She was taking a break from an enormous task of assembling years and years of family letters and photos into big leather albums. This is now called "scrapbooking," and the materials are delightful. The paper and stickers, even the plastic page-covers, are acid-free and will not fade the photos the way older albums do. I think I had better start to re-do all my own albums. That will certainly be a great project for snowy days!

We drank rich chocolate, watched a rerun of "I Love Lucy," one of her very favorite American shows, and had a fine time. Occasionally she handed me a photo, and explained who it was, where it was, etc. I was enthralled to learn that her family had summered on Bad Ischl, and knew some famous musicians of the day. Wincey remembers many summers at the lake, the concerts, the sumptuous décor of the hotel, the foods, the guests. But she speaks of it all with little bitterness. She knows how her life was forever changed by the Germans taking over Austria. She held up her left arm, pushing back the soft cuff of a mohair sweater, to reveal five gold bracelets. I had noticed them before, as she always wears them. This time, though, she explained that she had been wearing them the day she and her family left Austria, after Hitler's take-over. They were able to take trunks of precious possessions, like the photos, because the family had just packed them to store them upstairs. But most families were not so fortunate. Wincey sipped her chocolate, carefully setting the Meissen cup back onto its delicate saucer, and told me stories of her wonderful childhood in Vienna, and her life over here in the 1940s in St. Louis. It is amazing to think that she and I lived quite near each other! She is almost ten years older than I. Her first beau was killed in the war. She married an American, in the restaurant business, in 1950, and has only been widowed a few years. She moved to Colorado to be near her only grandson, who works in Denver now. He comes to see her every now and then. But I think she is lonely.

When I climbed the stairs to my own apartment, surrounded by so very, very many "remembrances" from the past, I cried. For her and for all older people with almost no one to share their stories with. What rich stories she must have in her! She remains one of the most lively, positive people I know. I have all of you. I have my health, my memory, my music, my friends, myself. So, as I sit in the winter kitchen and watch the Saints Windows across the way glitter in this bright day, I rejoice. I rejoice in my freedom. I share Psalm 30: 11, 12:

"Thou hast turned for me my mourning into dancing:

thou hast put off my sackcloth, and girded me with

gladness: To the end that my glory may sing

praise to thee, and not be silent. O LORD my

God, I will give thanks to thee for ever."

I will write again soon, dear.

My love to you both—

Mother

* * *

Jan. 24

Gordon P. Warner, Esq.
Attorney at Law
McComb, Horwath, and Faw
3267 Miniver Street, Suite 4
Denver, CO 80222

Dear Mr. Warner:

I am writing on a business matter, but not a usual one, I fear. This does not concern my estate, although I would like to meet with you sometime this year about some changes, so I can leave some kind of bequest to Knox College in Illinois. I have been meaning to do so for years.

I am writing today about my cat, Melodie. I have had her for several years. The management of the apartments claims to have sent all the tenants a notice to the effect that no one can replace a pet who has died or otherwise vacated the premises. I am certain that I never received this notice. I have been told that my cat violates the rule and I must get rid of her. I refuse.

Please advise me of my rights. I brought Melodie here after my former cat, Nepenthe, died three years ago. Nepenthe was a blue-cream Burmese, and I had brought her here from Sam's and my house when I moved here. She was never any nuisance here in my apartment; nor is Melodie! I personally believe that our management thinks it can intimidate us—most of the tenants are elderly women who have lived here at least ten years. I would like to keep Melodie, or any other pet I might want to bring in after she is gone. I like the company. Please advise me of my rights. Thank you for your help.

Ann C. Bow

P.S. On the estate planning: Do I have to decide anything about trusts for my grandchildren? My daughter-in-law asked me over Christmas, suggesting that I start to shift assets to her children annually. Lillabet Akers Bow means well, I'm sure.

* * *

Tuesday

Dear Wincey,

Just a tiny note under the door (I saw that your lights were out, and didn't want to phone or disturb you) to thank you for the cactus garden in the pottery dish. I saw it by my door when I came back this evening from dinner. I treated myself to some pasta at the little Pasta Pronto restaurant that just opened this month near the bookstore. I went alone, as it was such a fine, quiet evening, with the sidewalks cleared, and the old snow caked along the sides in such odd shapes.

Can you come up in the morning for some coffee? Say, around 9? I have a new machine I want to show you. It is becoming quite "high tech" in here! Once I really learn how to work this new gadget, we will both have much fun with it. I started to work on another psalm the other day, basically about control and dominion. I enclose it here for you. You are the first to see it. By the way, no need to bring any rolls or coffeecake—there will be "loaves" aplenty!

Fondly,

me

PSALM 3

... My domicile
awhile, in style,
in files and memories now,
the space once graced with those now gone,
embraced in thought, awhile, and smile;
pray, pray, pray for dominion

from opinion and place,
from space and domicile.
May this race be for grace,
Christ, styled after you.

* * *

Wednesday, Jan. 26

Dear Elise,

You will not believe what happened today. It has worn me out. The day started so well, with a visit from my neighbor Wincey. She left around 10. I was seated in the kitchen waiting for my new bread machine to finish another wholegrain loaf (the aroma is so much larger than the loaf!), when I heard loud knocking on the door, went to open it, and was confronted (!) by two men with a cat carrier, who proceeded to produce papers that gave them the authority to take my cat! I could not believe it. I moved to the phone to telephone the landlord, when one of them whipped out a card that showed he was an employee (God help us all) of the company that manages my building. He, to his credit, seemed apologetic. The other man enticed poor darling Melodie into the carrier by opening a can of food; they nodded to me, left a form letter for me to read, and left.

I am devastated. I just phoned my lawyer, and he is in court, so there is nothing I can do about anything today. Melodie! In the hands of strangers! She has lived here her entire short life ....

I suppose Melodie was not the only cat taken away today, come to think of it. Of the twelve or so tenants here, at least ten have cats. I hate being pushed around by rules. And, with my luck, my son will take this occasion to tell me for the hundredth time that I should give up my home here, and MOVE. Won't you please write or call, Elise? It has been so very long, and I know you must be tired from your trip, but I must hear from you!

Love and impatience,

Annie!

P.S. I don't think I have ever asked you this ... did you move Glenlivet to your new home? How has the little old pup adjusted to Arizona?

* * *

Wednesday, Jan. 26

Dear Ian,

I'm quite behind in writing you to thank you for our fun Sunday in the Springs the other day. I especially enjoyed the car trip this time. It so often seems as if a bright time is followed swiftly by a dim time ... and by now you may have heard my plaintive message on your machine ... but I was so devastated this morning by the men taking Melodie away that I actually wrapped up in a wooly gown, made myself some tea, and went back to bed, to recover.

I must have dozed on and off for an hour or so, because I was awakened by the noises of Mrs. Allenby vacuuming in the front rooms. I had forgotten that she was coming in the early afternoon this week. I'm afraid that, in the retelling of the tale, I broke down all over again, and both of us were crying before I was done! She is such a dear. And she has three cats at home. She truly understands how attached one can get to the dear pets. Charles, I might add, has never understood that at all! His son Adam has a little dog, but they keep it outside, or in the "mud room" off the kitchen, and, I must say, the little thing does have a dog's life!

That reminds me, mentioning their home, I have an update on Carson's situation. I got a letter from Lilla—quite brief, but more friendly than hostile—with the name and address of the place in Columbus where Carson will receive treatment. Carson has chosen to leave school for now, and to try to complete the program. I know that this is awfully hard on her ... just a week or so ago, I received a letter from her with her ballet program enclosed. I am sure that her passion for ballet, and the necessity of being rail-thin, are behind this eating disorder.

I know you are out of town, dearest, but I'd love a call and a visit when you return. When did you say it would be??? February 1st? Think of me, and think of Melodie, when you read this. Maybe there will be a way for me to get her home again!

Love,

Ann

* * *

Jan. 27

Dear Faye,

I called your home last night and got the answering machine ... so I decided not to ruin your return home by leaving a sad message to greet you. By the time you get this letter you will have been home about five days, since it seems to take about that long for mail to reach southern Florida! My darling Melodie was "collected" yesterday by employees of the company that manages my apartment building! They claimed they were merely following company policy. I have called my lawyer and he thinks they might have a chance of keeping her, at least until I and the other tenants meet to review the actual policy, etc. I called there today to make sure they had not put her away! I was told by a secretary that all the confiscated pets were being held together in a special section of a kennel. Imagine! I am going there tomorrow to get Melodie out, and to take her to my vet's, where she can be boarded until this is all straightened out. In fact, I am driving some other older ladies, all of whom are getting their cats out.

Today, dear, I am having lunch at "Librettos" downtown with Professor Thomas P. Jenkins, who is at an area community college. He seems most seriously interested in your father's unpublished music manuscripts. He called me before Christmas, and this will be the first time we will have actually sat down together. I will bring him back up here afterwards to go through some of the many boxes of papers I have kept in the storage unit. Mrs. Allenby (my housekeeper, have I mentioned her to you?) carried them up for me. I have told Alicia, and Charles, too (I think ...) about the man's interest. I have often wondered if your father thought that the music unpublished and/or unperformed at the time of his death were meant to be made available someday. It was one of the things we really never discussed. I have, of course, looked through the boxes and boxes of materials many times since his passing, if only to hold the old pages in my hands, to think back on the "creation days," as he used to call his bouts of composing, and to envision dear Sam's face as he worked into the nights on some new piece. He was actually working on something quite unusual before his passing; it was a collection of pieces for wind instruments and strings, that would combine musical ideas from three generations. I think he was planning to call it all something like, "Murmurs in the family tree." It was, I am certain, to have been dedicated to his three grandchildren. I wonder what Professor Jenkins will think of it? It was nearly completed, in fact.

Oh, Faye, thinking of grandchildren ... I know where little Carson is going to stay for awhile. It is an eating disorders clinic in Columbus, not far from the Worthington Inn, up north of town. Remember our staying there together several years ago when you and Austin came up for a bank stockholders' meeting? I was already there, visiting Charles and Lilla, and Carson performed in the youth troupe with Ballet Ohio. How many years ago was that? At least five. At any rate, this clinic is apparently in a lovely former estate, with gardens and reflecting pools, and pretty rooms, full-time counseling staff, etc. It is called "Pathway House," but I do not have its exact address, except that it's in Worthington. I don't think Carson is allowed calls except from her parents, at this point. I had Charles Federal Express me the information, but it has not appeared yet. I wanted to read about the place. Do you remember how you used to pick at your food when you were a teenager, and we were worried that you'd harm your growth by not eating well? Thank goodness, you never became ill, dear. Carson's situation is clearly a product of our television and magazine ideas of what constitutes a beautiful female form.

I have never had a weight problem, and I am thankful. I remain as slim as necessary, but I never think much about it. Some of my friends have not taken good care of themselves; some of them have smoked for years. But most of them have simply let their fitness and shape get away from them. The last time I saw Emily Evans she looked quite fragile. And Elise—whom I've not heard from in ages—was way too thin! Neither one seemed to be in great health.

Anyhow, dearest, I have rambled on enough. I am making sweet bread in my new bread machine, and plan to freeze several loaves to have on hand when I entertain Ian and his son next month. He assured me they would come to Boulder for a quick visit if they could fit it in. I was so pleased that you and Ian seemed to get along when you met at Christmastime. He travels a great deal, still. I wish he were home as much as he is away, but I am grateful to have him as a friend, at all. Few ladies my age have the attentions of an attractive, healthy, intelligent man.

Please send me some photos of the party you catered at the private school. What a job to make all the cakes look like different kinds of balls! I bet the tennis ball or the baseball were the easiest to ice!

I have enjoyed reading about your landscaping projects at the house, and am eager to see how you have swirled the periwinkles and groundcovers around the trunks of all those Norfolk pines in the side yard. I was terribly relieved to hear that Austin had security lights put in by the pool. Think "safety" and know that you are always safe in God's hands. The news of crime in Florida is awful, and we must pray to know that you and Austin and Lydia are always protected. Write me soon, dear.

Much love,

Mother

P.S. Here are some of the poems for young readers that I recently found in my desk ... thought some of your friends' children might like them!

"SUN"

THE SUN STOOD UP AND DREW HIS SWORD!

HE PIERCED THE NIGHT, WHO FELL AWAY...

THE MOON WAS CARRIED OFF BY CLOUDS,

WHO THEN RETURNED, ESCORTING DAY.

"THE FISHER MOON"

THE FISHER MOON HAS CAST HIS NETS

INTO THE DEEP, DARK SKY;

HE DOZED AWHILE UNTIL HE SAW

A SCHOOL OF STARS SWIM BY.

AT DAWN HE PUT HIS NETS AWAY

AND ROWED HIS BOAT ASHORE.

HE DREAMED UPON A MORNING CLOUD

'TIL HE COULD FISH SOME MORE.

* * *

Mrs. James L. Street
2327 S. Vermont Blvd. #32
Houston, TX 77074

Friday, Jan. 28

Dear Maryanne,

What a surprise to hear your voice this morning on my machine! I must have been out walking, as I try to do when the air is warm enough. And this was a glorious morning.

I would love to have you come by for a visit while you are in the area the week of February 14th to visit friends in Ft. Collins. I assume you will fly up, and there are several Houston-Denver connections daily. I'm not up to meeting planes at the new Denver International Airport anymore, frankly! But there is good limo service that will bring you right to my door. Perhaps your other friends might be able to drive down to get you when you leave, if they don't mind. It's not far.

If you could arrive here on Monday, February 14th, at the beginning of your Colorado trip, rather than on Sunday, I'll be able to see a little more of you. Sunday is a special Valentine Mini-Festival at the public library. It is a benefit for a local battered women's shelter. I am very involved with the festival ... I won't have a free minute until that evening. But I have nothing planned for Valentine's Day! Could you come then? Please feel free to spend several days! I have a comfy guestroom.

Hearing about your life in Houston will be most interesting. I have never spent much time there, although I knew San Antonio and Austin quite well at one time. My daughter Alicia, who lives in Boston with her son, David, attended Rice University many years ago, but I never saw much when I was there except her dormitory room and our hotel! I cannot now recall what year it was that you and Jamie moved to Texas. Alicia is now busy at a big advertising agency, where her specialty is designing materials for environmentally aware companies. I will show you a catalogue she did, using children from all over the world as models. Some of them are handicapped. I have something of a family situation on my mind right now, concerning my only granddaughter, Carson (Charles' daughter), but I don't foresee any immediate travel plans. I am certain to be here for the next month. I met yesterday with a music professor to look at some of dear Sam's unpublished writings. Busy, busy here!!

Please bring along that family photo/collage box that you wrote me about last fall; I would enjoy seeing pictures of your girls and your grandchildren. We can have a quiet Monday, and stay in. I'll treat you to some good food and good scenery! I spent part of this winter mounting old photographs and mementos against (copies of) Sam's sheet music, so that I could cover the wall in my guestroom with these three-dimensional lucite box collections. You will see them, but one of my favorites is the one that holds the tiny organdy and lace Christening gown that all my children wore, their three sterling heart charms, and several photos, all against Sam's "Cameo for a Christening." That piece, written by Sam for harp and bells, was, I was told, one of Benjamin Britten's favorite pieces.

Photography is not one of my talents. But a dear pal of mine, Ian Torrence, is quite the "photo buff." I have been reading about Edward Steichen (you know, the one who took that really famous picture of Garbo?) He shot many famous people–bankers, stars, writers–and was also known for his poignant, bleak photos of everyday people. Sort of a "Hopper" I might say, of the photography world. Ian has taught me a lot this past six months about the art form.

I have a loaf of *jalapeño* cornbread in the bread machine and the doorbell ringing, so I had truly better sign off for now, Maryanne! Call me, or write, with your final arrival plans. And by the time you arrive the library festival will be over, and we can just cruise smoothly into a new week. Your guest room will be ready for you! We have so much to catch up on!

Fondly,

Ann

* * *

Saturday, Jan. 29

Dear Charles,

What an interesting week I have had! In between hearing from my old school friend, Maryanne Street from Houston, and meeting a music professor downtown for lunch to discuss your father's music, I also heard from my lawyer that I will be able to bring darling Melodie back home!!!! You can't believe how very much I have missed her. The windowsills have been too bare; the rooms too quiet. I want her back underfoot. It is a fairly complicated legal issue, and seems silly, really. But the fact remains that the management company's pet policy cannot be made retroactive. I think I will be paying something like $500 to my lawyer. But he did save the day!

Have you any news about Carson? Have you or Lilla been able to visit her yet? May we write her at Pathway House? Or would it be best not to? Please advise me, dear. I thought I would get to work on a Valentine package for her (and one for Adam), but I will not include ANY food, don't worry. I thought I would find some books, maybe some stickers, some ballet knicknacks. I would love to send her some flowers ... would you see if that would be possible, Charles?

My foot/ankle are completely fine now, so please don't worry about me. My housekeeper is a big help, but I could manage without her. And don't give a thought to my tax affairs; I have, as you well know, a fabulous accountant and an equally good estate lawyer; between them, they keep me afloat. Tell Lilla there is no need for her to recommend that your Ohio people start to handle my financial affairs. I will be here ... not Ohio ... although I can count no fewer than four (FOUR!!!) different brochures in this week's mail from Ohio retirement communities. Charles, I wish you would have my name taken off that Orlando outfit's mailing list! Are you and Lilla actually familiar with these places? Of the four, The Park in Bexley sounds the nicest. You would not really want me that near, believe me. And I am perfectly happy right here.

Wincey is coming in a few minutes for some Kona, *madeleines*, and an hour of Michael Tippett. It is the kind of music I would love to share with Carson. Oh, my! Please keep me informed, Cat. And get me off that mailing list before Easter, or I might become angry! Ta ta, dear.

Mother

P.S. I just had a brilliant thought: why don't you put Austin's name, and his mother's name, on the Assisted Living Mailing List that is put out by Orlando's "CARE CLEARING HOUSE"? After all, Milli Wills already LIVES in Florida, dear ....

* * *

Jan. 30

Mrs. Leyman Carter
4123 Cedar Lane
Boulder, CO 80302

Dear Mrs. Carter,

Thank you for your note, which I received yesterday. I have not forgotten my promise to do a reading for your group, and think that the last week in March would be fine;

say, the 27th? I approve your selection of the Children's Library downtown and the idea of a little reception afterwards in the hallway over the creek. I hope your members will enjoy the event. They were so gracious to me last time. I will read from *The Canyon* and sign copies if you would like. What would you think of our having a little music with it? I have a harpist friend who is familiar with some of my late husband's music, and I can think of several pieces that would go very well with the poems I have in mind. My dear Sam would be pleased, I know, for his music and my poetry to be combined in that inspiring setting over the water in the very heart of Boulder! I can ask the harpist if she's available, if you would like. It would add a lovely touch. As for the publicity for this event, do whatever you and the Art Society wish, but I agree completely that a brief article in the weekly calendar section of the local paper and the Denver paper is a good idea, in addition to the bookmark brochures distributed by the libraries. And, in answer to your final question, yes, I do prefer to use my full name when I read, so it should be Ann Cunningham Bow. *The Canyon*, by the way, was printed in 1991. Thank you again for inviting me to do the program. If there are any more details that you think we should cover, what do you say that we meet for tea before the event? Just give me a call.

Sincerely,

Ann C. Bow

P.S. Here is one of the short poems from *The Canyon*

"STONE"

We climb on stone, sun-hot,

Silk-smooth, steep stone,

With knees bent and arms bent,

Climbing, clinging where we

Really don't belong.

Nor do we belong under the sea,

Or somewhere in the skies,

Armored in metal flying machines.

But when we see a slope, a wave,

A cloud, we dream: Ah, that I

Were there where I cannot be!

Come, lean against the hot stone

With me, with our feet forever

On hard ground. There will be

Time enough to climb when we

Lift towards eternity.

* * *

Monday, Jan. 31

Dear Members of Common Prayer,

We will meet Sunday, February 6th, 4 pm, at my home (26 Dover Lane) to finalize the plans for our mini-festival Valentine Day's Program at the library on the 13th. This is just a reminder, so that everyone will come prepared! I believe the following list explains what we decided at our last meeting. If you have any questions, please call.

Goal: to raise $5000 to renovate the bedrooms at the battered women's shelter, Havenhome.

Event: Mini-festival Sunday, Feb. 13th, with music, crafts, art show, food sales, readings from women's fiction … all to be held at the Public Library, main lobby and meeting rooms.

Tickets: Seniors (60+) $8; Regular $10; Student $5; Ten or more: $8 each

Time: 10am-4pm, no snow date.

Media: Jesse MacWhorter will contact the papers; Lynn Peterson will contact the radio stations; Else Santiago will contact public television stations. All press releases must be proofed by Tina or Don Schoeber.

Food: All sale items to be supplied (wrapped, priced) by church denominations who support Common Prayer's festival; Angie Ibin and Helen O'Hara to coordinate cakes, pies, breads; Michaela Marin to coordinate candy.

Art: Area high school art teachers will contact Mark Smithers by Feb.10th, about hanging art shows, pricing, security, etc. Art jury has been selected; awards will be announced one hour before end of Festival on the 13th.

Readings: I will coordinate readers, and work with library staff so that books will be available for check out.

Music: Professor Thomas P. Jenkins will assist with musical activities. More on this later.

Decorations: Have your Valentine boxes ready to be hung in library on Feb.12th. Lucite only; weight limited to three pounds. Common Prayer cannot be responsible for valuables ... for insurance info, contact Leslie Blackmore.

Shifts: to be discussed at meeting. Plan for two-hour shifts and please remember your buttons and the women's shelter brochures!

With enthusiastic fatigue!

Annie Bow

P.S. I will serve coffee and tea, and if we run into dinner time, we'll order something in, all right?

* * *

4 pm

Dear Wincey,

Just a quick note to ask if you would be able to come up tonight, say, about 7:30, to work on the Valentine boxes? I must get them done for the mini-festival. I will have Russian Tea and soup and fresh dill bread for our dinner, so don't eat before you come! We can sit by the window and talk without little Melodie racing around with a mouthful of ribbon ... but I hope to have her back within days!

me

* * *

February 1

Dear Alicia,

It is a blustery beginning of a new month, but already dark out. A chinook wind has rattled windows all day, and last fall's leaves are now in mounds along the walls, making the inner courtyard look messy. Melodie is back! She is by my feet. She has followed me from room to room all day. I have a big project to complete in the next week, for the Valentine's festival I'm in charge of at the library. But I thought I would take a little break and share my day with you, dear.

Do you recall my telling you about the lucite boxes several of us, in "Common Prayer," are making as displays for the festival? I was going to use fairly traditional Valentines as the backdrops in each box, until I asked myself what you might do! Your insistence on recycled paper inspired me to get out my tray and screen and scraps ... *Voilà*! I have spent part of today making my own paper, just the way you showed Lilla and Faye and me how to last year. I had your notes, and all has gone very well. The papers are different shades of rose; my favorite contains gold sparkles. And the textures!! I especially like these homemade papers when they feel stiff and rough, sort of like old tortillas. They are mostly dry now, and I plan to mount them, collage-like, in the five boxes I am responsible for. I have hopes to layer other objects so that the paper shows up well, but so that people have to peer closely to read or discern any words or shapes. There won't be any regular hearts in my boxes. I have had much fun snipping raggedy shapes from my box of fabric scraps, especially from the old skirts and placemats I have saved for decades. They are nearly translucent in their fineness ... much finer than they ever were in their heyday. Wincey came up the other evening for dinner, music, and snipping fabric. She has a real flair for seeing a special shape in cloth, following a wrinkle or a seam. She is a sculptor, with threads, yarn, silks, wool ... it is wonderful to watch. I have a fulfilled feeling about my Valentine boxes. I think they will speak to people, making them slow down, making them see more than is there. How I wish you could be here on the 13th! It will be a glorious day of festivities! And for such a good cause. The battered women's shelter here, Havenhome, is a place for healing, for rest, for prayers and dreams to be aired, and answered.

I will go to bed before too long. These windy chinook days take something out of me; I need to be deep under the bedclothes, safe and sated with psalms and wellness on these nights when the building shakes with gusts as if all the ghosts and witches of times past were circling my encampment. Goodnight, dear.

P.S. Isn't it exciting that David is interested in a prep school! I think it is great that he wants to apply to St. Christopher's in Richmond, as well as to several in Mass. and Connecticut. Your father would be so very pleased! You might also suggest Episcopal H.S. in Alexandria.

Mum

* * *

Tasai Manell
Dept. of Music
University of Colorado
Boulder, CO 80302

February 2

Dear Tasai,

I have not seen you in several months, but received a wonderful report of your recent concert in Silver Plume with the Cascade Players! A mutual friend of ours, Georgie Carrington, attended with her class of intermediate string students from Tarry Middle School. I wasn't sure if you had met them, or not. Georgie talks so fast I was not certain exactly what they all had done! But I had been thinking of you, in any case, for a project I am involved in on Monday, March 27th.

Let me preface all of this with an enormous apology, for not having been organized enough to ask you months ago ... but I did not know, myself, until recently that I would definitely be reading from my (1991) collection called *The Canyon*. While discussing some of the details the other day with Mrs. Leyman Carter, who is organizing the event, I suggested that a musical accompanist might be perfect, and I thought of you. I wondered if you would be interested in playing several of Samuel's short pieces for harp? You might prefer to perform the same ones you chose several years ago for the church service in his honor five years after he died. What do you say that we meet for lunch soon, if you are interested, to work out the details. Let me know what your fee would be; this group of art patrons has a healthy budget.

Fondly,

Ann Bow

* * *

3 pm Thursday

Wincey—

If you can come up around 4, I have something to show you before I get it all wrapped up to mail tomorrow! I discovered a new shop downtown, and can't wait to share with you what all I found! Most of it is for Carson, but some is just for you and me and our afternoon teas! I will give you a hint: it is old-fashioned, needs ironing, and will remind you of grander times, when people dined at mid-day, supped at night, and sometimes had a small repast late at night after the opera ....

Ann

* * *

Feb. 3

Dear Carson,

I have, as you see, enclosed this letter in the surprise box for Valentine's Day. You may open the box as soon as you get it, or wait till the 14th ... GrammyAnn will leave that up to you.

I won't comment, now, on the goodies inside. I think they are things you can use while at Pathway. Your father phoned recently to say they had seen you, and that you have a lovely room that looks out over treetops. They told me that Adam had been on the winning team for his after school basketball competition, and was looking forward to spring so he could start some outdoor sports.

What kinds of fiction are you reading these days? I could send you some of my favorite books, if you would like. I have to weed through my possessions now and then, or they start to take over my life. I have some old editions of books I enjoyed when I was younger. I have re-read several of them over the years. When I was about your age, some of my friends and I had our own book club. We would all go to the library once a week, usually by bike on a Saturday, and select one or two books each. When I was quite a young reader I loved the adventure series books like the "Honey Bunch" series about a little girl and her escapades, and the Bobbsey Twins, of course, and all the Nancy Drew books. By the time I started boarding school, in Chicago, I was reading Dumas, Dickens, Conrad, Balzac, Scott, and Cather. And I have not stopped since! A favorite recent novel for me is *The Stone Diaries*, by Carol Shields. I hope you, too, are a reader. Reading is the very best kind of "vacation" one can ever have. Next time you write me, please tell me who some of your favorite authors are, all right?

Take care, dear. I am always here if you would like to write or call! Happy February!

Much love,

GrammyAnn

P.S. Dear, I keep forgetting to ask you or Adam, but have you been reading these new "Harry Potter" books?

* * *

Friday, Feb.4

Mrs. Peter Evans III
11 Crow's Peak Court
Colorado Springs, CO 80906

Dear Em,

Thank you for your note. That stationery from Kansas is exquisite! I had never before seen corn and grain silos painted as abstract objects, and the colors were good enough to eat! If you were ever to run across more of the stationery, I would happily pay for at least three boxes. (You know what a hoard of writing paper I have.) I read with much interest the little "bio" on the back of the cards. Imagine a woman in her eighties deciding to keep her family farm by turning it into a seasonal artists' colony! What a great idea! Elena Riviera Moetta can really capture a mood.

Thinking of interesting uses for old buildings, I'd like to tell you about a shelter (for victims of domestic abuse) that used to be a home. I am in charge of an event at our library, on the 13th, that will raise money to renovate the bedrooms. We will raise the money from baked goods, crafts, book sales, etc. for Havenhome. Did I ever tell you how I became involved in Havenhome?

I am a founding member of a group called "Common Prayer," that includes women of many religious backgrounds, including Islam and Judaism (although there are more and more evangelical Christians). We meet every few months, usually at someone's home, to talk about one political, one personal, and one religious issue. Yes, Em, this is a serious discussion group, that quite surprises some of my newer, young acquaintances, who think that I, being in my mid-70s, should stay home and watch tv re-runs, I guess! Several months ago we were discussing national security, personal safety, and spiritual well-being, when a quiet young woman said that she had been a battered wife for years. She explained that she had lived at a battered women's shelter, in Virginia, until she had earned enough money to move away. She has been in the Boulder area for about four years. She asked if we knew about Havenhome. Most of us had read about it at least once, but none of us, I am ashamed to admit, had ever thought of it as a place we could become involved with.

Havenhome, like so many special shelters, has no listed address or phone (for security reasons). But we received permission to meet with the executive director, for a tour of the facility, on a day when the residents would all be away on a planned excursion.

As soon as we saw the place we knew we wanted to do something for it. The woman who gave us the tour was a lean, articulate Black woman of about fifty, who looked you right in the eye when she talked, and had laugh lines around her own eyes. She was remarkable. She had almost single-handedly founded the place (also formerly a small family farm!) after a neighbor's daughter had been nearly battered to death by her husband back before these things were much discussed.

The house is a three-story frame structure with a wide front porch. There are twelve rocking chairs on the porch, and each one has a tiny plaque on the top with the name of the donor. Naturally, I peered at each chair, out of curiosity, and was amazed to see that about half of the chairs had been donated by area physicians, and the other half by area church groups. There is an airy front hall, with a big flower arrangement on a table, but no mirror. Feleecia explained that most of the women do not want to see themselves. It takes months for self-esteem to return, even though they were the victims of abuse, not the perpetrators. Several of them have their children with them.

There is a big dining hall, with a communal bench, like a refectory table in a boarding school. Otherwise, the room was bare. A living room held several worn couches and chairs ... nothing really matched, but they were just mismatched enough to slightly daze the eye. Upstairs there were, on the two top floors, a total of ten bedrooms. You could see that big rooms had been divided. What caught my eye, in particular, was that the rooms needed painting (or papering). The twin beds were plain and covered with thin spreads. I asked Feleecia if people regularly donated things like sheets and towels to Havenhome, or if there were some kind of fund or endowment or something out of which such things were bought. She just smiled. She said that occasionally a local charity would donate a set of towels, etc., but that funding depended on individual donors and grants. She is in the process of setting up a cooperative crafts guild, in which volunteers and residents can work. (quilting, crocheting, sewing, etc.) The Guild will market their items downtown to start with, and then try to have a Web page. My! I did not know what one was, and I had to ask during the tour. I am becoming very modern, Em. One either adapts or one gets left behind in the dust!

We (Common Prayer) are going to raise $5000 to spruce up the bedrooms. Then, we hope to plan another fundraiser for this coming year to start an endowed fund for the place. To do this, we will have to meet with Denver groups, and I wondered if you knew anything about interest for this sort of project in Colorado Springs. Come to think of it, we might as well ask all over the state. I bet there would be people in Aspen, Golden, Ft. Collins, Vail, and elsewhere who might like to be part of this enterprise.

You and I had talked about getting together soon. I think Maryanne Street from Houston will be here next week for a day. What would you think of your coming up sometime during the week of March 10th ? Let me know! I will be pretty busy from now until this "do" on the 13th, but after that, I will be home, resting.

Fondly,

Annie

P.S. Directions to my home:

Take highway to the University exit and take University Blvd. to shopping area on The Hill, on the left, and turn uphill. Come to corner of Cartesian and 12th.

You will see Dover Terrace tucked away on your right. I'm in the wing of the building that faces Cartesian. You can park anywhere on the street.

* * *

Morning of the 7th of February

Dear Elise,

I actually phoned Ramsey View today, hoping to reach you, since I have not heard from you in many weeks. I reached an operator in the main building who said there was no answer in your unit. I almost NEVER call you, as you know. I assume you are on the road. What trips you must have been enjoying since before the Christmas holidays! I hope you are not completely worn out! Is Jeff keeping you hostage somewhere??

One reason I am writing, aside from the love of writing you, is to send along several poems I have recently written. They are to be part of my new collection—at the publisher's right now, in fact. I am calling the collection *Moving Day*. It has so many possible meanings, that I won't subject you to my own private one! You know me well enough (perhaps you alone, actually, as time passes) to know that I like my life here. If Charles and Lilla realize that someday, I just might be content!

An aside—do you have ANY idea how many retirement communities exist in this country? I am learning. I receive, usually, no fewer than two glossy brochures daily, from the retirement clearing house in Orlando (thanks to Charles). I admit that some of them are breathtaking in their locales and amenities. As I am certain your very own Ramsey View in Arizona is, dearest, although I haven't heard all about each tiny detail of cuisine and comfort! The wise thing for me to do, and I realize this of course, is to put my name on a waiting list at one of these places, in an area I would enjoy being in. Then if and when I get to that point in my journey on the narrow sidewalk of Life, when the cracks are too wide and the pavement too uneven for me to skate along merrily and safely, so to speak, I will have a place to call home where I can be cared for without bothering my family.

The chinook has finally let up; we have had days of that non-stop howling. I have had to come and go quite a lot this week, arranging things for two separate library programs. It is the wind in my face, and the wind gusting so that I feel jerked back and forth when I walk, that disturb me. I have nothing against wind, itself! Ever since I was a very young girl I have thought of the winds as being the West Wind, East Wind, and North Wind. (I never heard of a South Wind, did you?) I see them all as huge, cumulus faces with puckered mouths, blowing and blowing. One blows dust and sand, one blows a fresh salt breeze, and the last one blows cold air and flurries. But a chinook just blows! What kind of wind do you have in southern Arizona? All I know about your part of the state is that hummingbirds pass through on annual migrations. Perhaps we should all feel like those hummingbirds, Elise. Vulnerable, delicate, strong, determined, colorful, and always on the move!

I am enjoying February with a new black caftan, a cookbook that emphasizes fat-free cooking, olive oil, and grains, and the return of my darling pet Melodie. My kitchen windows are nearly gold with dust. It has blown into each room. My housekeeper had never seen such a wind, and she has not kept on top of the residue! As I sit here with a pot of almond tea, I see that my feet have rubbed circles on the floor, and that my cotton dress has a hem lightly speckled with golden dust. I am wearing the weather, it seems! As long as it has not mixed in with my new flour, sitting right here awaiting loafhood, I won't mind. When I finish this letter to you I will toss the ingredients into my machine, and have a fresh loaf of peasant bread by dinnertime.

I envy you your travels, yet at the same time, I envy myself my being home in my home. Does that make sense?

Here are some of the new poems ... let me know what you think of them, all right? I always appreciate your comments. You weren't an editor most of your life for nothing!

Annie

ENTERTAIN

I cannot fold them in my arms
or make them phone
or tell them how I need them all
when I'm alone,
for obviously they never dwell
on things they've never asked about:
do I need help, or company,
someone to hold the ladder steady,
or to call me when a meal is ready?

So I love them as I will, and must,
in the only way they seem to know:
what to them may be but an evening out,
a meal at my home instead of theirs,
a chance to dine with someone else,
becomes for them an assumption:
"She entertains a lot."

How often do they even know
the etymology? To entertain: a way to love,
"to hold or keep among," in short,
the heart and home and hope of
Hospitality.

*

SUMMERHOME

There is a place where paths cross
once a summer, if we walk away
from our houses in search of sunflowers
twice our height on the schoolhouse road.

We can see Little Traverse Bay
through a gap in the pines on the bluff:
this is what I seek, not someone, but a scene:
like the days of childhood summers.

Here is the land of the Chippewa,
French fur trapper, and Jesuit missionary,
land fought over by the British,
waters fished by the Indians,
and seen in early stories by Hemingway.

His family, like ours, journeyed
northward to flee the heat of the Illinois plains.
Walloon, Charlevoix, Petoskey, Bay View,
We-que-ton-sing, Menonaqua, Cross Village,
Harbor Point, Harbor Springs, adieu....

Farewell, summer home, birch woods, cold waves,
place where paths cross once a year.
I left the house key, locked the doors,
packed my pennants and camp banners, my dreams.

Only I, the child, can still race to the water
or run through the dark woods on the bluff.
For I, the adult, must now move on, released,
by the end of a vision, not the beginning of one.
Hunt me, Chippewa dream warriors,
carry me to your next hunting grounds someday
so my spirit can play, can play, can play ....

*

TRIPTYCH OF LIFE

Pass
from the silent preamble
through gold and coral-colored shores
on a nine-month journey
to be born and held
immediately, crying.

Pass
past everyone alive
in your lifetime
doing unto others
what you would have them
do unto you, and
seek longevity and peace
or heroism and grace,
smiling and loving.

Pass
into a cone of noise,
press stars
onto your palms;
lie against the beginnings with

only an echo of
chaos remaining. Then
turn your eyes downward
as you move through new
gold and coral-colored shores
to meet
the gaze
of some
dolorous staret.

* * *

Feb. 7

Dear Ian,

A very quick note to send along a fairly old poem of
mine, that I unearthed today when I was hunting for papers
in my "project closet." I remember writing this poem after
Sam and I spent a weekend at the old Arlington Hotel Spa
in Hot Springs, Arkansas in the 1970s, when the woods
were lush with magnolia blossoms. I wrote Elise earlier
today, and ended up having the most restful time here alone,

enjoying the quiet and baking. I thought of you loping around Golden with company, and hoped you both had a bright, cold beer and enjoyed the brewery tour. So glad that you are back in Colorado. See you soon, love!

Ann

BEYOND THE LAST SPA

Never the leisure of lying
in linens,
tended by staff
with trays of tea and foreign papers.
Not
I. I
forge ahead
alone along
the path that climbs each hill,
magnolias above, mosses below,
so that the view is
behind
me.
I know
I would
be
a pillar of salt
if I turned around.
God knows what
I'd be
if I ever turned back.

* * *

Tuesday, Feb. 8

Dear Charles and Lilla,

My! What a weekend! I am tuckered out, but happily so. Melodie and I are lying on the sofa in the front room looking at the clouds and listening to folk music. I think it was one of your records, once, Charles.

I guess the old *cliché* that no news is good news applies. I have heard nothing new about Carson, so I pray that things are going well. I imagine that you went out to see her yesterday or today. But, as you said in your last letter, visitors are not encouraged if the patient is depressed. Is she depressed? Or is she overwhelmed with all the pressures of missing school and ballet? I do hope her school is cooperating by not assuming she will "make up" missed classes, and so on.

I heard from Faye yesterday. She sent a little mini-album of photos of their new landscaping. It's quite an ambitious endeavor, with all sorts of tropical plants on trellises, new trees, and lawns that curve in all directions. She has to weed everything herself, for now. Austin says they cannot (yet) afford a groundskeeper. She said that much of the old real estate down there is undergoing a big change as new owners buy the smaller "early Florida" bungalows with the white roofs, *lanais* and pools, and yards dominated by ancient banyan trees, and tear them down to put up two or three-story mansions. The result is that there is almost no room between the homes anymore. I think her new landscaping plans are one way to help give them more privacy now that neighbors on both sides will have multi-tiered houses with views down into Faye's yard.

Lydia is very much a presence, if I read correctly between the lines. Faye mentioned, briefly, a small incident in which Lydia had an all-night "slumber party" with about eight of her high school friends, at the house, but that about ten boys joined the party around 2 a.m. Austin apparently laughed it all off, and Faye is still too hesitant with Lydia to know quite how to handle a small gang of Florida teens! I don't envy her!!! She made them all leave, which I think took a lot of courage. I applauded her.

I have been busy, myself, lately getting everyone and everything ready for the Valentine Festival on the 13th. We all met here on Sunday for several hours. Everyone got along well, but there is always some friction when there is a group with so many very different personalities. The arrangements are in place—everything from publicity to insurance. They are good volunteers and I am very much looking forward to next weekend. I wish you could see the Valentine boxes! They are stunning. It amazes me to think of the variety of materials and design displayed. My own feature home-made paper and shaped fabric pieces, suggestive of the glorious natural and spiritual evolution, if you will, of Love itself.

I have also been busy getting poems together to be included in two separate collections, the psalms, and the one I'm calling *Moving Day*. I have so enjoyed working on these poems again. Some remind me wonderfully of earlier joys; others are responses to recent moments. If you would ever like to see any of them, let me know. I have made up several little packets to share with close friends, and can easily send you one. Do you think Carson might like some of them?

I am thinking of all of you. I hope your February in Bexley is not too severe. It has been terribly windy here, but there has not been much snow for awhile. Tell Adam "hi" from his GrammyAnn, and save some love and hugs for the two of you and sweet Carson.

P.S. I'll have a houseguest from Texas on the 14th

Love,

Mother

———Clip here for Quiz Questions for Adam———

1. What colleges/universities are located in: Galesburg, IL; Hancock, MI; Jacksonville, IL; Williamstown, MA; Lexington, VA; Charleston, SC; Huntington, WV; Winston-Salem, NC?

2. What is the difference between "etymology" and "entomology"?

3. What does "Père" mean in French? Who was Père Marquette? Where is he buried?

4. Why did you miss the question about the northernmost country, in the other quiz? Don't you have an atlas? I gave you one last year. Try to find it, dear.

5. In what towns are these colleges: Central State University in Ohio; William and Mary in VA; Harvard in MA; Southern Methodist Univ. in TX; Occidental in CA, and Miami University in Ohio? Where is there another university with "Miami" in its name?

6. Name three American rivers that begin with "M" and three European rivers that begin with "R."

7. Name four towns along the old Oregon Trail.

8. Name six Native American tribes.

9. What was "the long march" (Indian history), and which tribes were involved?

10. Ask me a question, Adam. I will answer in my next letter.

* * *

Feb. 9

Dear Alicia,

Night has arrived, and with it a light snow. I hope it clears by the weekend, so that our festivities at the library go forward. We need to attract a large crowd if we are to raise $5000.

I hope to get the developed film back tomorrow morning of the lucite Valentine boxes I made. I want you to see my very own homemade paper.

Another, smaller, project I undertook recently was to concoct a Valentine box for Carson. I sent it in care of her parents, and hope she will be allowed to receive it. I feel so sorry for her, being away from home in that facility. Yet I know from reading the materials Cat sent me that she must be in a structured program if she is ever to cope with her eating disorder. I wonder what her days there are like? It is probably a feeling of homesickness, like I felt when I went away to boarding school.

In the box, which was a hatbox of mine, that I decorated with paper flowers and hearts and then laminated, were several packs of stickers, showing dancing animals, flowers, and some bears. I enclosed a package of pink stationery/ drawing paper and three felt tip pens, a cassette tape of folk music, and another cassette of her grandfather's piano music. I added white pants (we used to call them pedal pushers when you were a child) and a tunic top, suitable for wearing inside to meals, etc., and a small purse of different shades of red and pink, with a $5 bill inside. Do you suppose there is anything to spend money on at Pathway House? Books, paper, pens, anything?

Guess whom I saw Sunday as I was coming out of the Canyon Creamery? Katya Gillespie. Do you remember my telling you about her visit here, her disdain of my home? She is impossible. I don't know if she is trying to insult me, but she was shrill and strident, walking up to me to ask, loudly, if I wanted to join her and her friend at the Château Country Club next weekend for dinner, or would I be "too busy with all the artists and gay groups?" I ask you ....

Let me know what you and young David are doing. Would you, or he, like to come out here for a visit for his spring vacation from school? Since he missed his winter visit, perhaps he would enjoy a visit in April. I think March will be filled with working with Professor Jenkins on your dad's music manuscripts, and with finishing up the editing, with the publishers, of my *Moving Day* collection. They want to publish the book of psalms next year, so I am not worrying the process! I did, however, pen one the other evening, while I enjoyed a cup of almond tea and some

challah bread and your father's "Melody for I. M. Pei." Here
is the new psalm, dear. Let me know what you think.

Mum

I SHALL BE WHOLE

I throw myself
at your hem, Lord,
hourly in my day,
knowing that my faith
illumines how I pray.
"If I might touch but
his clothes," she said,
"I shall be whole."
You felt that power
go out from you, Lord,
and she was healed.
I am that woman, too, now
knowing you walk my way.
"Go in peace," you told her.
I, too, go in peace, and pray.

* * *

Feb. 10

Eleanor Bascolm
Editor, Mt. Elbert Press
3124-A Monmouth Street
Denver, CO 80222

Dear Ms. Bascolm:

I received your query today, and wanted to respond
immediately, as I will soon be tied up with a library program
and a houseguest. I was most pleased that you had been told
of my work by Jan Adelsson Carpenter, whom I have known
for some thirty years. I last saw Jan at a conference at the

University of Denver. I was flattered that she mentioned me to you. By the way, I'm doing a reading from my work on March 27th at our public library.

I am preparing a collection of "psalm-poem essays" on spirituality; I have completed most of them. And, finally, I am writing an introduction to my late husband's music, as a new anthology is to be published this fall by our University Press here.

My book of poems, *The Canyon*, was published in 1991. I would enjoy meeting with you to talk about your press and some of its projects.

Sincerely,

Ann Cunningham Bow

* * *

Feb. 11

Dear Tasai,

Thank you for your note (and your new home mailing address in Englewood). I was sorry that you will not be able to play at the poetry reading on March 27th, but very pleased that you would like to arrange a similar program at a Denver library later this spring. You can count on me!

Everything here happens at once! I have a houseguest arriving Monday, for whom I am ready. And I had to pop into the library quickly to see that my committee members were getting things ready for this weekend's mini-festival. And, in the midst of all of this, I met briefly today with the woman in charge of the program I had mentioned to you. (I think my children think I sit in a rocker all day!)

It was a rather odd meeting, actually. She has been trying to get me to read for their arts group for many months (I did a similar program for them before), but when we discussed details today, she very pointedly suggested that I not offend anyone. She then alluded to having heard that I now attended Table Mesa Baptist, in her words, a "church of the religious right." Ah, Tasai! As a Catholic child I lived through years of discrimination, some almost too subtle to be seen by non-Catholics, such as the way Protestants could "assume" you were poor because Catholics were "always poor." (Needless to say, I was a child LONG before the Kennedy clan and the immigration of a Cuban elite made Catholicism more "acceptable.") Immediately, immediately, I realized that she was "embarrassed" for me, (and of me?) Perhaps she feared that I had written a poem about abortion. I smiled and told her that my poems are written, and stand as they are, but that only someone looking for a fight would find fault with any of the ideas. Poetic language, as I write it, should be comprehensible to all English speakers. Poetry, like music, may reflect cultural ideas and trends; but that is quite different, I think, from catering to ideas and trends.

I write as a mind ... as an educated woman, a widow, an American (of Celtic and Dutch descent), but as a MIND, really. You, as a musician of African and Indian descent might have a different individual experience of United States culture, yet we have been exposed to the same events and trends, and share a cultural vocabulary. Our lenses may be different, but we wear the same kind of glasses, and can focus them on the same thing. Does that "thing" have to appeal to everyone equally? Inclusiveness demands that we speak or create only in ways that could never offend anyone.

Well! See how agitated she made me? I look forward to our working together again soon.

Let me know which library will be best for us to set up our performance, and which dates work best for your schedule. I have very little planned for late April, after Easter, or May. Take care.

Best Wishes,

Ann Bow

* * *

February 12

Managing Director
Assisted Living
Ramsey View
Monte Vista, AZ 85324

Dear Sir or Madame:

I am writing in the hopes that you will be able to give me some information about a dear friend of mine, Elise Parker, who resides in Unit 6. I have written her quite often since just before the Christmas holidays; I have tried to phone several times. It either rings and rings and rings, or the line is busy. I even phoned your office once to ask your operator to ring her apartment, and we got no answer. I have not received any mail from her, either. I assume(d) she is on a trip, but I am beginning to get worried. It is not like Mrs. Parker to be out of touch for so long. I tried to phone her son, but there is an answering machine on his line. The "beep" is so long that he must have many, many messages waiting for him. I assume he is out of town. In fact, he and his mother may very well be traveling together. But I am getting worried. I have known Mrs. Parker for decades. I am enclosing a little card with my phone number and address, for you. Please let me know if you hear from her, so I can put my mind to rest. Thank you.

Sincerely,

Ann C. Bow

* * *

Note to myself, or to give to the Art Society if necessary (late evening, Feb. 12th)

- We may ignore age, accent, skin color, and gender preference altogether much of the time, as they are not relevant to the situations at hand, be they board meetings, musicals, or drama productions.

- We may appreciate an opera when the singers are good,whatever their ethnic background. Or a play if all the actors are good. But if a director were to insist upon an all-Black cast for "The Marriage of Figaro," or an all-White cast for "Porgy and Bess," or an all-Chinese-American cast for "Oklahoma," an all-White cast for "Raisin in the Sun," or an explicitly lesbian cast for "Little Women," then, I think, it becomes absurd, because then, the color or gender DOES get in the way.

- Does our creative work have to appeal to everyone? Are we allowed, anymore, to respect our own unique experience and to recreate it in our creative expression? Some of the members of the board of the Art Society are afraid that my writing will offend a young, non-white, non-native-English-speaking, or gay, or non-religious audience.

- Imagine what some of the greats, like Donne or Rilke or Pound or Auden would have said to these issues. What are we coming to?? Exactly WHERE is my "freedom of speech" anyhow? Which freedom of speech issues capture all the interest of our media?

- As a writer I have a right to express ideas. I do not write for a particular audience any more than Sam wrote for a particular audience. Our ethnic backgrounds, cultural identities, and personal taste can either be highlighted in our work, or irrelevant in our work.

* * *

Feb. 14
Dear Elise,

Happy Valentine's Day!!! I just tried phoning you this morning but got no answer. I have even written the management of Ramsey View, hoping to learn of your whereabouts! It's not like you to be so hard to reach! If it has been a trip you have been on, I know it has been a splendid one! I remember a trip Sam and I took in the mid-1960s, to Scandinavia. I made a point, a selfish one for me, of not writing anyone except the children. I missed them terribly. But it was an important trip for Sam; he got some ideas for water music from the fiords and waterfalls. And after spending hours in Vrogner Park in Oslo, with those magnificent, huge statues of families and children, he wrote his "Outstretched Arms Symphony," which has been compared to Dvořák's "New World Symphony." It premiered at the University of Wisconsin the next year, and we went.

It's been a busy week here. Maryanne Street arrives today, from Houston. I spent yesterday at a wonderful Valentine Mini-Festival at the library—a fundraiser for Havenhome.

I have the guest room ready with a little basket of Colorado postcards next to the bed, in case she (or any other guest—hint, hint—how about a visit!) wants to write anyone. Luckily, the winds are not too strong today. That room can be quite noisy because it's a corner room, and the wind seems to pound it. Maryanne lost her husband not long ago, and this may be her first solo sojourn. I want to make her feel completely at home in this cozy, comforting haven. I would have done more for her arrival, if it had not been for all the time the festival took.

I wrote you about Carson being at Pathway House in Columbus. I haven't really heard much. Charles sometimes phones and leaves a brief message on my machine. I don't know why I always seem to miss his calls!

You remember Sally Hinson, who used to run into you and me downtown. She is now living in Florida, at a place like yours, near her daughter. She wrote the other day to say she was having such a wonderful time in her new place. She has stopped driving, too. She even takes the van to Mass on Sundays, which is quite a change for Sally, who used to boast about getting church behind her on Saturday afternoons! She rides the van to the local Publix Market and seems to enjoy her new lifestyle.

She told me such a funny story. There are quite a few people in her new community who like to know everything that is going on. As she says, they do not "miss a trick." So she invited lots of the people she has met, at Bay Reef Cove, to a holiday party. And she told everyone that she wanted them all to meet a brand new couple, from "up north," who had recently moved in. When the day of the party came, there was quite a large crowd, as everyone was dying to meet the "new couple from up north." Sally had them all in, served some eggnog, chatted with her friends. They had all been looking around, curious to locate the new couple, and to "check them out." Sally went over to the drapes that cover the big glass windows to her patio, pulled the drapes, and stood back. She then said, pointing to gigantic (5' tall) INFLATED figures of Santa and Mrs. Santa seated on patio chairs, "HERE is the new couple from up north!" Everyone just died laughing! Isn't that a fun story?

Is life at Ramsey View similar? All kinds of people? Is there a good supermarket nearby? Sally eats one meal a day in the dining room, and said she usually fixes her own lunch up in her apartment. She always loved to cook. I love to cook, too. But you never really did! How is the food there?

I hope that your long silence just means that you have been on a trip and are too busy to have caught up with all of your mail! I am truly looking forward to hearing from you, you naughty traveler! Can't wait to hear about your journeys!

I am going to wind this up now, dear. I have had such a very full weekend, and I am trying to catch up! I would never tell Charles this, but sometimes I do feel tired! Part of it is simply the stairs here. I seem to run up and down them a dozen times a day. But I'm still glad that this apartment is on the second floor. I don't think I'd do well without my daily view of the Flatirons.

Love,

Ann

P.S. How I wish you could have seen the Valentine boxes, heard the music, eaten the pink and red foods, and spent time with us at the library! It was splendid!

* * *

Wednesday, February 16

Dear Wincey,

I found this doily in my Valentine things and sewed it onto a piece of red velvet, for a very special "thank you" for the beautiful Valentine tea you had for Maryanne and me. I was so touched by your attention to details—the iced heart cookies, the music, the embroidered linens, the elegant tea tray with the sweetheart roses for us! I think it fair to say that you, my Viennese friend, have truly mastered the American Valentine *Fête*! I have seldom enjoyed a more gracious occasion.

Wasn't it great fun to hear some of Maryanne's anec-dotes about St. Louis? The two of you overlapped in St. Louis, and might well have seen each other, without know-ing it! I loved her story about the 1904 World's Fair, or I should say, correctly, the World Exposition at St. Louis in 1904! To think that Geronimo was there, and was actually seen by her parents! I had no idea that the 1904 St. Louis Exposition had been held to celebrate the 1803 Louisiana Purchase. I will have to concoct several "Grammyann Quiz

Questions" for Adam and David, from this new knowledge of mine!

I had forgotten all about my own family's part in that Fair. A long, long time ago, when I was just setting up house with Sam, my father showed me a lovely, heavy, elaborately carved crystal pitcher. Dad told me that this pitcher sat, never used, on a sideboard in his parents' home. When he took my mother there one day, in 1908 just before they were married, she put some water and wildflowers in the pitcher. He said there was an appalled hush when his parents came into the dining room and saw what she had done. No one had EVER used this pitcher, because it was famous: it had been the pitcher that won, at that Fair in 1904, "Best American-made Crystal Pitcher!" The Cunninghams explained to Miss Alice Ann Capps that they had bought the famous pitcher in St. Louis at the Fair. When my grandparents passed away, it was left to my parents, and then, later, to me. (I gave it to Faye when she married Austin, or I would show it to you.) Just think, Geronimo must have seen it! An odd juxtaposition of cultures. I just love that kind of thing! Ian will love to know that Geronimo was at that Fair. He has told me stories of Geronimo and copper country in Arizona, and how Geronimo even marched in Teddy Roosevelt's Inaugural Parade. Amazing, simply amazing. That was not all that long ago.

When I came back to the apartment, I found that the florist had been here. Alicia sent a white azalea with a pink bow and Faye sent six white chocolate roses! I was touched that my girls remembered me. This has been a very comforting week so far. Hearts to you, dear one!

Ann

* * *

Feleecia MacGregor   February 16
Director, "Havenhome"
P.O. Box 3235   Ann C. Bow for
Boulder, CO 80302   Common Prayer

Dear Ms. MacGregor,

It is with our warmest thoughts, and hopes for the recovery of women staying at Havenhome, that I, on behalf of our Valentine Mini-Festival sponsored by Common Prayer at the public library, give to you this check for $4800. This should help to refurbish some of the bedrooms, and we look forward to doing more for Havenhome in the future. We had hoped to give you $5000, and we will try to round off the amount with a few individual donations soon so you get the full amount.

Perhaps the Valentine Mini-Festival could become an annual event? I would not always be one of the main organizers. But Common Prayer might continue to be the sponsor. Please keep sending your "Wish List" to each of us sponsoring churches, and we will see that it runs in our church bulletins. I know that you need more bars of soap. Would the hotel travel-size bars be all right? I know that most people tend to take extra, unopened ones home with them when they travel. I think I will put out a basket, here at my apartment building, and at my church, and ask everyone to drop their travel bars in! I will see that you get them, probably by the end of March. As for some "extras" like sofa pillows, vases, platters, I will see what some of us can do. I have a neighbor, as well as several friends, who can sew, crochet, and quilt. (Those are not skills that I have.) They have asked me to ask you if they could begin to make quilts for each of the beds at Havenhome. They would love to meet with you sometime to discuss this.

Again, many thanks for all that you do for our community.

Sincerely,

Ann C. Bow

* * *

Thursday, 6 p.m.

Wincey—

Can you come up for some dessert around 8:00? There is a special on television, about Austria. It is going to focus on the cities, art, architecture, and music. It would be enjoyable for me to see it with you. I did not know about it until a few minutes ago, when I switched from The Weather Channel to PBS. I knocked and heard some water running, but did not want to bring you out of the kitchen. I could become addicted to the weather news! I love a storm. The bright red-orange blobs moving swiftly across the screen are so interesting! I don't want a storm to hurt anyone, obviously. But just to watch its course, its shape, its colors on that channel is extraordinary. Just imagine what a difference such information would have made to explorers trying to cross an ocean or to map a continent!

I am still unwinding from the weekend, and have to admit that I am pretty worn out! The best part for me was watching the people look at the art, talk about the Valentine boxes, and to respond to the readings. It does my heart good to see a crowd turn out for something other than an athletic event of some kind. No one ever gets crushed to death rushing into an arts festival, do they? Thank Goodness.

By the way, the dessert tonight is something else Faye sent me lately. I think you will like it! I only drink decaf, as you know, after six pm., but this new decaf she sent is so smooth. It is "water washed," whatever that means! It is a label from her shop, and is called "Sand Dune Blend." Isn't that attractive!

Your Weatherwoman and Crazy Neighbor

Ann Cumulus Rainbow

* * *

early, early a.m. Friday

Dear Wincey,

I awoke this morning with a peacefulness due to our conversation last night about your stories and descriptions of Vienna, Linz, Salzburg, and Melk. Weren't those scenes from Vienna just delightful? The red streetcars gliding by like big fish, the church steeples, the lush gardens in the many parks, and the specialty shops filled with umbrellas or fine pastries made me want to get right on a plane and head on over. I finally remembered the name of the little hotel where Sam and I stayed in the 1970s when he was a guest lecturer at the Universität Wien: the Alpha Hotel, near the American Embassy. We had a gabled room, quite small, quite reasonably priced, considering the inflation then. A charming European breakfast was served in a bright room overlooking a tiny garden, but the hotel did not serve other meals. The Alpha was not very far from the Votiv Kirche. St. Stephan's was completely covered with scaffolding that year and all one could see was the zig-zag mosaic roof. The photography last night was stunning, and that church looked glorious. I have told you about my course in German at the University. Thank you for saying you will help me brush up on my conversational skills. I have not used my German in many years, except to try to read something occasionally. Just to read a poem, like *"Der Einsame"* ... what joy! Only Rilke has ever captured the essence of "loneliness," wouldn't you agree?

I will be out much of today, and probably unable to catch you in the hall to thank you in person, so I wanted to tuck this note into a tiny "thank you basket" for you to discover when you open the door later this morning for the newspaper! It seemed only fitting to give you some *Kaffee*, as the Viennese were among the first Europeans to enjoy it. The beans, by the way, are lightly flavored Amaretto from the Canyon Creamery (remember, they have specialty coffees on Wednesdays?), which I picked up when I tracked down seven-grain flour for my bread machine. Inside the foil there is a baked apple (just add a dollop of cream); and inside the linen is a small loaf of "GrammyAnn's Best Bread" for you, which I made and froze several days ago. By the time you read this note the loaf will have thawed.

Sit by your front window and look out at what will become a windy, bright blue morning, and think of the blue enamel of those Viennese stoves, the peal of the abbey bells of Melk, the birds gathered at Türkenschanz Park on a crisp day, and think of me, a friend who relishes your every reminiscence!

I am up early to get several tasks done before I leave for downtown. I am meeting with my banker this morning. I'll fill you in later. It's an idea I had recently that might make my day-to-day life simpler. I got the idea from my friend in Florida who has set up a special account to pay her bills for her.

I am listening to some music for Celtic harp, "Silver Apples of the Moon," by Ceoltoiri, three women with much musical talent. Samuel would have loved it all. How sad I am that he never knew public radio's "Thistle and Shamrock," for he would certainly have wanted to weave the sound of a Scottish harp into one of his melancholy pieces. If we had listened to more radio we would have found this program. This is this time of day that I miss him most keenly. The mountains have a stripe of red in the lighter sky, and every sense I have is tuned anew for the smell of the coffee, the pling of the harp, the roundness of the orange grated into a custard, the silkiness of cake flour, the gift of day. And when I walk beside the creek in a few hours it will help me, grandly, to know that my home here has nourished me well, and will nourish my friends.

Thank you again for an inspiring evening. Enjoy your repast (and drop by for the orange custard at tea time if you are home) —

Danke vielmals,

Ann

* * *

Saturday, Feb. 19
Dear Charles and Lilla,

I received your letter in today's mail, and am grateful that you are keeping me up to date about Carson. No, I have not been home a great deal lately, as I have been involved in a festival, and have had a houseguest. The festival was a big success last Sunday. I regret that I missed your call Sunday. I was probably still at the library.

At any rate, I have very mixed feelings about your apparent decision to let Carson leave Pathway House after only two weeks of treatment. Surely, that is not enough time! What could they have done for her in a mere two weeks? Are you really sure you should let her return to school? What do the counselors say?

Does your health insurance cover any of the cost? This kind of treatment must be frightfully expensive. I hope you don't belong to some HMO that will not pay for anything! Pathway House has the amenities of some of the assisted living communities, truth to tell, that I am forever being bombarded with. The communal dining room there looks very attractive, light, airy, pretty.

Pathway House has a mission, a purpose for Carson. If you are all displeased with the place for some reason, I would like to know. I will do anything I can to help find the right place for my only granddaughter! Please accept my help as help and not as interference.

By the way, I had an old college friend from Texas, Maryanne Street, here for a visit early last week. I have another friend coming March 4th, but we can easily change her dates, as she lives in the Springs. I am available to come to Bexley if you need me. I am feeling fine, and might be of some help to you around the house, or whatever. Please call me if you need me there.

I have gone to the library recently and have read quite a bit about eating disorders. It seems like a modern phenomenon, doesn't it? One book I found especially interesting, and perhaps of interest to you for Carson, is called *Food for Thought: Self-Nurture and Nourishment for Recovery*. It is written in the form of a daily diary. This quotation from it might help all of us right now: "Valentine's Day is, for most Americans, a day of rich chocolate in satin boxes with red bows. For us, it must become a day of rich nurture of the soul, when love so fills the heart that all in our day are blessed ... but without candy. Give a heart-shaped box filled with pot-pourri or costume jewelry or herbs. Accept gifts graciously, but give all candies away immediately."

I will try to find you a copy of this book, for it has something most helpful to suggest about each holiday. Frankly, until I read it, I had not been conscious of how very food-oriented our modern culture is! Think about the foods we associate with each of our special days, including birthdays. I will definitely find the section on Easter, for Carson will probably be at home, won't she, April 25th? *Aloha*, sweet ones. Keep me posted. Keep me in your hearts.

Love,

Mother

P.S. Cat, I do not have a dishwasher, and I really don't need one, dear. I kind of enjoy washing each plate and glass by hand, and I get them thoroughly clean. Don't give it another thought!

* * *

Late Feb. 19

Dear Ian,

Your call warmed me. You understand how fragile we can feel when it comes to our grandchildren. My letters to

Charles always seem to cross with his calls, and it is as if our words to each other, like silk lines thrown by spiders, entangle with each other, and neither web is secure. Does he even know of my worry? Carson, from the vantage point of my years, is a child with her whole world before her. To him, she is a daughter with a blighted future, like a dancer maimed by a fall. Yet her fall has been a terrifying spin downwards through the dark world only she really sees. She needs time to lie still, very, very still, I think. Only then will she be able to stand the light. Your embrace over the phone, and your promise of a visit next week, give me strength. God alone has the winds in His fists. We need to grasp what time we have, and shape our lives, spending our hours and money where our hearts lie, and not fall mere victims to the flow around us. Thanks for understanding my eccentricities dear one.

Ann

* * *

Sunday, Feb. 20th

Dear Maryanne,

This letter should find you safely home in Houston. I so enjoyed your visit! I used the freesia glycerine soap log this morning in my bath, and am saving the lovely oatmeal soap for later. Can you believe that it has already been almost a whole week since you arrived??

I am enclosing a clipping from the local paper, to share a little of what last weekend involved for me and Common Prayer. I think it is a favorable summary of our efforts on behalf of Havenhome. With this kind of good press, the shelter should be able to attract more donors. Something not in this press clipping is a remark I overheard from a teenage girl, looking at the lucite heart boxes. She said, "It looks like love has been captured here ... like butterflies pinned under glass."

Maryanne, you know what a rambler I am; before I forget to tell you again, I was enthralled by the photo collages of your family. You have put a lot of work into those, and they are worthy of their own display in a museum. Your granddaughters seem, by their photos, to have been allowed to develop almost like wildflowers, expressing such unusual traits and talents, wholly unique and imaginative, so unlike the rigid correctness required by Lilla, or so it seems to me, for Carson. Your girls have let their girls be themselves, as if they were so confident of their daughters' directions, that few guidelines seemed necessary. And the pictures of them over the years, the pictures of the girls aswirl in linen drapes and strands of tiny stars, or bursting from concentric water waves in a dark lake under a full moon: those pictures make them seem one with nature. How I wish Carson were like them. She dances, it is true. But her very disorder and her sadness are tolls she pays for not being at peace with her world or with herself. I don't mean for this to sound like a *cliché*, but I wish she could know she is not dancing a dance, but IS the dance.

Your visit has inspired me to rummage through my boxes and to try to assemble mood collages for myself. Sam could do it with his music. I think I have tried with my poetry. But your pictures set these thoughts out to be seen, not heard. My poems and Sam's music are food for the ear first, then the heart. Your photos and pictures speak right to the eye and the heart. I am ready! I have learned a lot about the beauty of photography recently, thanks to my gentleman friend Ian Torrence.

Call me sometime when you have a chance. I understand that you prefer the phone to a letter. And if you miss me, I will get back to you soon. My poetry reading is now scheduled for March. Otherwise, I am simply riding out winter, like snow on a pine bough! Thank you for coming to stay.

Love,

Annie

VALENTINE MINI-FESTIVAL

Sunday saw our public library filled to the brim with the good, the glad, and the curious as local women's group "Common Prayer" successfully attracted hundreds to a Valentine gala featuring readings, foods, crafts, and art displays. A benefit for the local battered women's shelter, Havenhome, the Affair brought some $4800 in, to be used to upgrade the bedrooms. Of particular interest were the prize-winning paintings by area artists Leanna Toquay and Jon Peterson, the music, "Strings for Streams," written by the late Samuel T. Bow and performed by the Student String Ensemble of area high schools, and the varied Valentine boxes, created by members of Common Prayer. The boxes will remain on display in the corridor over the stream for another month, thanks to the festival coordinator, local poet Ann Cunningham Bow.

* * *

February 21st

Dear Alicia,

I am resting! The festival was a success! We raised $4800. We also got good press coverage. I was pretty much worked to the bone. I also had a very pleasant visit, afterwards, with my old friend Maryanne Street, who had flown up from Houston.

Three of my main volunteers begged off, apparently sick with a bug. But our Common Prayer committee members rallied. Professor Jenkins assisted with the Student Strings, who played your father's "Strings for Streams" quite well. The art show was hung nicely, and the judges selected two very different winning paintings. I did not particularly care for either of the paintings, but you know my taste. I'll take a Cassatt or O'Keeffe anyday, over some muted display of gray streets or photo-perfect fruit. But the public was happy.

Maryanne and I had not seen each other for years. She is a new widow, and this was her first big trip without Jamie. She had also planned to visit friends in Ft. Collins, and they came to get her Tuesday. I met them, had them up for coffee. I'm not sure quite what they thought of my apartment ... but I think Maryanne liked it, maybe even envied me a little, as she has a big condo to take care of. She said it holds every piece of furniture they ever had in their house, because she just could not bring herself to give anything away. She used to live in a very modern, one-floor house. But she told me that she did not want to be there alone. Why she moved to a condominium, at her age, instead of one of the lovely assisted care communities in her area, I do not know. As long as she had been planning to move anyhow, she might as well have opted for a place with a health center and communal dining room. As it is, I gather that she eats out quite a bit at a club. I do think she enjoyed the coziness of my little home.

She was here such a brief time that I cannot really make a judgment about what she is like anymore. We have been friends since the 1940s, although she left Knox College before she finished, because of the War, you know. Lots of women students had to drop out, either for financial reasons or because a brother had been sent overseas, or had died in the War. She had come from St. Louis. She made a "good marriage" with James Street, raised a healthy family, and is truly enjoying her grandchildren. She has become a true "Texan," full of news and politics from the Lone Star State. I think she probably used to play golf, bridge, and do some medical volunteer work. Poetry and art are not big interests, but I rarely find anyone for whom they are! She and I are actually quite alike, in spite of outward differences in hairstyles, taste in clothes, and in homes. Maryanne, like so many of the ladies I know and see everywhere, wears her hair very short and permed. Her clothes are well-made, but in colors and fabrics that I rarely choose. I love linen and cottons, caftans, classic suits, a blazer. She dresses more for the club, in bright print separates that end exactly mid-knee. Her shoes were bright flats, but did not look very comfortable. She likes monograms. Let's just say that I am more "Bohemian!"

We have shared interests in music, design, and travel. But she and her husband, and often their children, usually took planned tours, cruises, and the like. We have been to many of the same places abroad, for instance, but have quite different memories of them. She might have played golf at St. Andrew's or at Troon, whereas I sought out short lecture-tours around Glasgow's art galleries and museums. She had been in Venice several times, and Florence, but usually to shop for lace and linen and glass. I took an Italian cooking class in a restored palace. You see what I mean. But it is challenging to bring two perspectives to a place in the past, or to specific shared times from college years. And we did have some great laughs over our fun, little trips to Chicago on the train back in the 1940s! We always tried to fit in a visit to the Chicago Art Institute, which, as you know, is still one of my very favorite museums anywhere.

You should see her photo collages of her family! Collages are her main artistic interest, and she is good. They are masterpieces. I showed her some of my new scrapbooking materials, and she is familiar with them. We talked late into the night about the necessity of pinning memories down, of saving rare moments. I talked quite a bit about your father's music, and his philosophy of giving permanence to experience. I did not show her much of my poetry, although I may someday send a few poems along. I was pretty bushed, actually!

Her visit clearly brought a question to my mind, one that has fluttered on the edge of becoming a poem for quite some time: what happens to us when we are guests in another home? Do we truly bring our entire selves into that home? Or do we share only that which we think will be tolerated, or appreciated, or not criticized? I sensed in Maryanne a person more complex, perhaps, in her visions and values, than she is permitted to reveal on a day-to-day basis with people at home. Her daughters and granddaughters are astoundingly imaginative, but lead quite separate lives from Maryanne. And Maryanne seems much like a Chinese puzzle box—full of mysterious secret drawers and treasures, but ones not accessible to everyone.

I have another friend coming in early March. I am looking forward to it, but I kind of wish I had not planned the two visits quite so close together! I will get the guest room ready for Emily. I want to put the new flannel sheets with the bold stripes on that bed. Emily is very particular about fabrics. She is a decorator-manqué! Her letters always mention something tactile, like pima cotton, or damask drapes, a chenille robe. I sometimes have taken her descriptions right out of her letters and entered them in my writer's notebook, because they are so exact, so charming. Listen to this one of a new linen smock: "made from hollow flax fibers, it is extraordinarily strong given its weight, and is sandwashed, soft, with invisible seams." She actually sent me that (I was able to find it a minute ago after rummaging through a hatbox of her letters and snippets of fabric) one year. I almost asked her for the smock! I did write a poem based on the fabric ideas, and I enclose it below.

I have not heard from Elise for ages. Having Maryanne here, and having Emily about to visit reminds me that I am fortunate to have such friends. Wincey is the unexpected gleam on a piece of old silver: she is a marvel. I only hope some of my life enriches theirs, as much as their lives do mine.

Dear, I nearly forgot—I'm meeting with my lawyer soon, to discuss some charitable gifts, royalties from the music, possible income from my book, and a trust for my grandchildren. I want everything to be fluid. Nothing irrevocable. I wanted you to know, especially since Lilla and Charles have been after me for months to use their accountant and estate attorney in Bexley. I am satisfied with my own, as I have told them. My riches, in essence, are things not of this world. But let me know—all of you let me know—if there are particular THINGS you might like to have someday. I will put little tags on the furniture, so no one need argue someday about the tables, the pictures, the art works! I don't mean to sound mortal! But feeling fairly tired tonight, these things came into my mind. Oh—I am certain that I will leave you all the Indian rugs! That makes me very happy.

I think I will settle on the couch now with some almond tea, a vanilla candle in a jar, and the lights off. The better to see, I think. The better to see.

Goodnight, dear

Mum

SPINNING LINEN

I am linen and silk,
sandwashed with
invisible seams,
draped carelessly onto a hanger,
arms raised and hands over my head
in a triangle on the pillow,
my chest soft buttoned pockets
and sleeves of hollow flax
fibers without cuffs
rolled up past the wrists.
When I wake after sleep there are long moments
when I know not who I am and
faces spin until my own comes into view.
I rise and put myself on for the day,
like a linen shift or silk trousers
without seams.

It is as if my soul admits for now
to being a banner readied to be flown
in celebration of this day
for which I have been
perfectly sewn.

* * *

Feb. 26

Dear Ian,

I left a message on your machine a few days ago, but as
you have not phoned, I thought I had better drop you a note
with the news. (I can't remember where you are.) I was
knocked down the other day! On the Hill, by a teenaged
boy. He kicked me, tried to take my bag, but didn't get
anything. I'm in bed with some herb tea, the lights on, and
Melodie. I don't want Charles to know, or Alicia. They'll
think I can't take care of myself. Call me when you get this,
ok? Wincey is going to mail it for me right now. Missing
you—

Ann

* * *

February 28

Dr. Peter Mills
2198 Arapahoe Square Suite 2
Whole Health Medical Center
Boulder, CO 80302

Dear Dr. Mills:

I am feeling quite a bit better since the attack on me last
Wednesday, and wanted to thank you for coming right over
to the Emergency Room at the hospital. It had been so long
since I had been ill or needed to consult my doctor, that I

had not realized that Jim had retired! However, now I know who the Jim was who sent a postcard from Christmas Island last spring! He does so love to fish! He and his late wife, Irene, used to bring Sam and me mountain trout ... ah, so long ago.

I am pleased to get to know you, although I would not have chosen these circumstances. I did not have any of my medical information with me when they took me to the ER, and I cannot thank you enough for having your office take care of the Medicare card, insurance information, and medical records.

I will make an appointment soon to come in for a follow-up visit, but the aching has pretty much ceased.

Have a good Spring!

Best Wishes,

Ann C. Bow

* * *

February 29

Dear Emily,

I just got your lovely note. I'm glad you are eager to come up to Boulder! I will be ready to receive you by March 10th! Just give me a ring if something comes up, or if the weather gets bad and you don't want to make the drive, and we will reschedule.

I have spent the past few days, believe it or not, recovering from a mugging! Yes! I walked down to the Hill to do a little last-minute shopping, and right there in front of the stationery store, a teenaged boy knocked me down, tried to grab my purse, but could not get it off my shoulder, and then kicked me! I got a good look at his face! It was dusk, and no one came to help me at first. Maybe they thought I'd just slipped and fallen. But when he kicked me,

I screamed. Then some people came over, but by then he had run off! The police took a statement from me, but they told me I was naive to be out on the Hill at night. I guess I've been lucky! Apparently, there is quite a lot of this kind of thing, done by high school students! Where do their parents think they are?

I am staying in a little more right now; my ribs were bruised, but not broken. Think of how my son would react if he knew I were lying in here because a boy tried to rob me in my own neighborhood! He would find some way to become my Power of Attorney, probably, and relocate me to a lovely assisted living home near them. I will just lie here and let my side ache a bit, and pray. Not so much for myself as for the boy who does not know right from wrong.

Love,

Ann

* * *

March 1

Mrs. Harold D. Hinson
Bay Reef Cove, Phase II
2428 S. Ocean Blvd. # 312
Boca Reef, FL 33446

Dear Sally,

I have had more fun telling people about your holiday party for the "couple from up North!" I think it is so funny that you are keeping them inflated and in your guest bath tub! What does the cleaning lady say? I realize she speaks only Spanish, so I guess you will never really know what she says! If I lived in Florida, I would be in deep trouble, as I do not have a single Spanish phrase, either. All those years of French serve me well in restaurants, but otherwise ....? I am glad to see my grandchildren learning Spanish.

This is our birthday month, isn't it, old girl? Let's not count how many years have gone by. Most of them have been wonderful, wouldn't you agree? You and Hal and Sam and I had many fun times out here. Every now and then I walk past your old home and think of those days. Real estate out here has gone through the roof, as you know. I am lucky that there is rent control at Dover Terrace, believe me! If there weren't, I probably would have to move in with one of my kids until I had a real good plan!

March will be interesting for me this year, as I have a poetry reading coming up, and a houseguest arriving from Colorado Springs in about a week. It has been windy. I keep busy with my projects. I am glad to hear that you volunteer in the Bay Reef Cove Library, and that it is not very far from your door. Isn't it terrific that people who live there can zip around in those golf carts, inside the buildings! That certainly is better than relying on a wheelchair or a walker or cane. Luckily for me, I can still navigate well. Your arthritis sounds like a real challenge, Sally. I am glad you are well-cared for down there, and that your cute daughter is only a township away. I envy you having a grandson old enough to come by and dine with you in the dining room. It must be gratifying to be able to "show him off" to all the residents, which is exactly what I would do if Adam or David dined with me in such a nice environment.

Thank you so very much for keeping in touch. There is almost nothing that I look forward to more than getting a nice, fat letter (with unusual stamps) in my daily mail. I just love the most recent stamps you used, those tropical orange flowers: Bird of Paradise, Chinese Hibiscus, Royal Poinciana, and Gloriosa Lily. (See! I have saved each one!) I tried to find some here at our Post Office, but they were sold out. I settled for the pretty fruit stamps. Good enough to eat!

Have a good month. In like a lion, out like a lamb. I love
what you said you were going to put on your door today,
that cute little lion. Gives me ideas. I think I have a lamb
around here somewhere for the end of the month. Take care.
Keep writing, Sal.

Cheers,

Ann

* * *

Thursday, March 2
Dear Lilla,

Thank you for your note updating me about Carson. I
am glad you decided to keep her at Pathway House a little
longer. I hope that they will turn her thinking around so
that she can return home and pick up her life again. How
considerate of her school to let her make up any missed
work by getting it done before May. That should give her
enough time, if all goes well.

I did not mean for the little quiz questions for Adam to
cause any controversy. I have such a love of geography and
maps, that I just like to share my enthusiasm with everyone.
Adam is not too young, at 12, to read an atlas. I meant no
harm. I had not realized he had not done too well on the
new Standards Test for his grade level in Social Science. I
wish I could see the questions. Are you, as parents, allowed
to see them? I would think that any practice he might have
in looking up towns and rivers, and the like, would help
him, not hurt him.

My, but his after-school life sounds busy. Do you and Cat
really take turns driving Adam to his various activities each
week? How interesting. Sam and I did not do that kind of
thing for the children, because they did not have activities
like Adam's available back then. I seem to recall that they

had PE right after school, and the sport would depend on the weather and season. Then they would either walk home or ride the school bus home. Parents were never invited to practices or even to games.

When I was in boarding school, of course, our sports were quite competitive, as we were always playing some other girl's school in something: soccer, basketball, volleyball, tennis, hockey, golf. Our uniforms back then were knee-length tunics: yellow cotton for autumn and spring, and black wool for winter. Oh yes, we had to play outdoors! Seems like we played field hockey until our breath froze on our cheeks! There was nothing quite like a cold wind off Lake Michigan to put some spirit into us! Some games were finished with amazing speed!

But I did not mean to digress. Adam has soccer tryouts, then baseball tryouts, Boy Scouts, private tennis lessons, and a Junior Cotillion class once a week, as well. When does he have time to do any homework? Or to play outside with his neighborhood friends? Was Carson's schedule as demanding? Surely, dear, your own younger years were not quite as packed full of activities after school, were they? Aren't you simply exhausted? Thank you for the photo of you all by your new SUV. I see a great many such large vehicles here, too.

I was interested to hear about your Financial Planner, and that she would like to discuss your future expectations as she helps map your investment strategy. Cat was never much interested in keeping track of financial matters, so I assume he is pleased to delegate this to a professional. I switched from one brokerage firm to another the year Sam passed away, so that I could work with someone who had respect for me as a woman investor. When Sam was alive, our broker always directed all of his remarks to him, and never even looked at me. Sam, dear thing, never noticed. I have confidence in my new man, and don't pay a whole lot of attention to anything but my monthly statement. So many of my widowed friends, here in this town and in their retirement communities, simply have no clue about their own financial affairs. I find that appalling. Luckily, I keep my weekly expenses fairly simple, and don't have the worry of credit card debt.

How sad, how predictable, to see all of the "For Sale" signs stuck onto almost new cars and trucks, as people everywhere (certainly here in Boulder!) have found that they have outspent their resources and have to sell that "extra" car or truck. Everyone is trying to keep up with everyone else. One would think that lifestyle really is all that matters anymore to most people. How very sad.

I have been quite busy myself. I am practicing for my upcoming poetry reading. It is almost like a musical performance. I want to be able to recite the works without looking at the page very often. That takes discipline. I am still enjoying my bread machine, and make a loaf several times a week. They are just the right size for one person. Melodie has been listless of late, and I worry about her. Cats just don't communicate as well as dogs do when they have a complaint.

Ian Torrence is fine. Thank you for asking. He comes and goes a lot, as he has friends all over. And he has a granddaughter in California who is about to have surgery. He may even be out there right now. I thought it amusing that you and Cat asked me the same question his son, Don, asked Ian recently: "Would you ever remarry?" I am sure that you have heard that happily married men, when they are widowed, either remarry within a year or two, or die. Of course, widows are tougher. Very few widows, happily married or not, have quite that destiny. Some remarry. But sometimes it is difficult, after being happily married, to find a man who quite measures up to one's late spouse.

I think a small choral group at my church wants to sing one of Sam's pieces. It is lovely, almost like a chant. He never gave it a name. But if it is to be performed, I will give it one. It has never been performed at any church here that I know of. We have about seven small singing groups at my church. Two of the groups are for teenagers to sing in. One is for much older people. I always forget to ask you both if either of the children attends a Sunday School, or a service somewhere. One of the most attractive features of my own church is their Family Center, with its many programs for youth. I often try to go to one of the Winter Dinners. There is a very brief sermon, a delicious meal, and some music, often the teen choir, "Fishers of men," performing contemporary music. It is a wonderful way to spend a Wednesday evening. I know very few people at the church yet, but I don't even need to know people, just to be in the room with them. That is "fellowship" enough sometimes, in a nice way. You and I have never really discussed "religion," yet I would think that having some kind of spiritual or church "home" might be of some help for Carson. Permit me to share a verse or two for you to cut out and give to Carson (or mark for her in Psalms):

> "... As the hart panteth after the water brooks, so panteth my soul after thee, O God. My soul thirsteth for God, for the living God: when shall I come and appear before God? My tears have been my meat day and night, while they continually say unto me, Where is thy God? ..." (Psalm 42: 1-3).

Charles was raised as a Presbyterian, as you know. But he stopped attending church years ago, possibly before he had even met you. I think his college years, in the early 1970s at such a huge university, when so many things were turned upside-down in our culture, what with an unpopular war in Vietnam, the unfortunate and tragic killings at Kent State, and Cat's own worries about the draft, all contributed to making him "pull away" from certain institutions. Church was, I fear, one of them.

You were still far too young in the 1960s and 1970s to have many memories of those times, I am sure. When you two were married in 1984 the world had settled down. You gave Cat a secure and happy home, and for that I thank you. See if you can't talk to him sometime about the children and their going to church. Columbus has a vast variety of churches. Surely something would appeal to him and to you. Do it for me, will you dear?

I am going to settle down with a cup of tea and some music now. Keep in touch.

And thank you, Lilla, for asking me to write you. I have enjoyed it.

Fondly,

Ann

* * *

Saturday, March 4

Dear Wincey,

Just a quick note to say that I will have a guest here on the 10th from Colorado Springs.

Her name is Emily Evans. She spent Christmas with her son and his family in Kansas City and has promised to bring along some of the photos from her holiday. I would like her to meet you, and for you to meet her. She is good company. Every now and then I drive to the Springs and we have lunch. I wanted to give you some advance notice, so you might try to hold an hour or so open in the late afternoon. I will probably take Emily out for dinner afterwards and try to catch up on news. I have been dining at home so much lately, I would like a little change.

I got a call this morning from Margaret Davis. I had not heard a thing from her since she left to stay with her son near Denver. She was admitted to Northeast Nursing Home last month and called to give me her phone number. She wants to stay there. Remember, she thought she would have to move to Tennessee to be near a son? This place she is in has full nursing care, a communal dining room, several public lounges, a television room, a van to take them on outings, and a terrace where residents can sit on a nice day. She said all the smokers go out there, so it is not too pleasant most of the time! Her Medicaid papers came through. Sure enough, Wincey, just as the grapevine said, a person on Medicaid has to sign over her income to the facility, and cannot have more than a small amount in a personal bank account. The Social Service people actually check from time to time! She said some people have abused the "system," by having assets to pay for private care, yet opt for a Medicaid situation, like Northeast Nursing. To keep that from happening, the rules state that a person can have only a small amount of personal income. That does not bother Marg much, as she told me she has only her Social Security check and a small pension from Mark's job in the Boulder Public School System.

She had a few funny anecdotes, too. It seems that one woman will soon lose the privilege of having a small microwave in her room, because she has been using it to dry her underwear ... and she started a fire! Imagine! Another person sneaked so many rolls from the meals and hoarded them so successfully that she created a roach infestation that closed down a whole wing of the place! Now, Marg says, no one can take any food from the dining room. I told her I would send a "care package" immediately! Maybe you and I can cook something up for a basket that we could take to her this month. That would be interesting, anyhow. I have never been in a facility that is classified as "Medicaid Only." I'd like to compare it to some of the ones I have brochures for. My, but most of those places are elegant!

I have rambled on and on, as usual. I will give you Marg's phone number as soon as I find what envelope I wrote it on. That is the trouble, for me, with the telephone: one is never really expecting a call, and when one gets a call and has to write a message down, one grabs whatever scrap of paper happens to be handy! In my case, it is ALWAYS an envelope. I hate to think how many letters I have mailed that have mysterious scribblings on the inside flap. Hmmmmmmm.

Cheers!

Ann

* * *

Tuesday, March 7

Geoffrey N. Parker
334 Carlin Ave.
San Francisco, CA 94114

Dear Jeff,

I am overwhelmed and devastated by your news. I don't think I have ever been so undone. The news was so unexpected. However are you handling it? I send you my deepest sympathy and love. I considered your mother my closest, oldest friend. I should have suspected that the long silence was unnatural. But whenever I phoned Ramsey View, no one told me anything at all, and I assumed she was either traveling or with you.

I think that they were waiting, as you said, to reach you, and you alone. Does NO ONE have any common sense anymore? You had been put down as next of kin, obviously; but why, oh why, didn't Ramsey View try a little harder to find someone to notify? I can only imagine your own terrible shock this week upon learning of recent events! Jeff, my prayers are with you. To think that her stroke was just before Christmas, and the poor dear was confined to a health center, all alone, and we did not know. Thank you for returning to me the large packet of unopened letters dating from December. Oh, Jeff, I am so sorry. I cannot believe that she never saw any of them. I just can't believe that she is gone. "Rules." "Privacy." "Bureaucracy." What do such words mean, anyhow, when a person's life is fading away!

Do not blame yourself! It is not your fault. Your being away on a trip was not some kind of selfish waste of time, as you hinted to me earlier! Your mother was happily settled into an excellent assisted care facility, one of the nicest in all of Arizona. You had every right to leave home for awhile. Who possibly could have suspected that dear Elise, who seemed in such perfect health, would succumb suddenly to a stroke? None of us had any idea that such a thing could ever happen to her, of all people! I just assumed that she was visiting you or on a trip. She had told me several times that, once settled in at Ramsey View, she hoped to take a cruise now and then. All of this time I have been picturing her on a ship. Here it was you who were on a ship thinking all was fine because you had heard nothing, either. Oh, Jeff, don't blame yourself. I hope those people can explain to you why her phone rang busy sometimes! What did they do, take it off the hook?

I will drop this in the mail today, and then try to phone you this evening when I am more composed. I needed to put something on paper first. That's just the way I am. By the time you get this letter, some of my shock and numbness will have worn off, maybe to be replaced by grief, or by tears. Right now, my eyes feel as if they are propped open, too far open, as if they are stuck. I have not been able to cry yet, but I know that I will, soon. Know deep in your heart that I considered your mother my dearest friend, and am devastated by our loss.

Your mother will live forever in my love for her.

Much love,

Ann Cunningham Bow

P.S. I will make myself available to come to California, if that is where you will have a Memorial Service, dear. If you would like me to arrange anything here in Boulder, where so many of your mother's friends live, I will do so immediately.

* * *

2 p.m. Tuesday

Wincey,

I am putting this under your door at 2pm, because I can see that you are not in. I will go back upstairs and make myself some hot, sweet tea, for the shock and chills of what I have heard today. I have had a terrible blow. I got a call a little while ago from the son of a dear, dear friend. You have heard me speak of her often—my darling Elise. She is gone. She had a stroke months ago and just died. I'm not very good company right now, and I need to be alone, yet I wanted you to know what has happened, because I know that you will pray for my peace of mind. Poor, poor Jeff. He is not much older than my Faye. This is awful for him. What an icy, rainy day of black news. Thank you, dear friend, for being here in our building, and for being a friend.

Ann

Wincey, I have been studying Psalm 42 all week, not realizing that I would need it so much and so often:

"... O my God, my soul is cast down within me: therefore will I remember thee from the land of Jordan, and of the Hermonites, from the hill Mizar. Deep calleth unto deep at the noise of thy waterspouts: all thy waves and thy billows are gone over me. Yet the Lord will command his lovingkindness in the daytime, and in the night his song shall be with me, and my prayer unto the God of my life ..."

* * *

March 8

Dear Ian,

I am in for the day. I am iced in by the outside, and iced in from within. I left a message on your machine last night. Elise is dead. Gone. Unbelievably gone forever.

You know I hardly ever say that someone is dead; I say "passed away." But I got a call yesterday from her son Jeff. He had been in Australia and at sea much of the time. He was out of reach now and then, he said, but fully expected that someone from Ramsey View could be able to reach him, somehow, if there were an emergency with his mother. And he got home last week only to learn that his mother had had a bad stroke shortly before Christmas, had been taken to the health center, and then to the hospital, and finally died last week. The fools FOOLS FOOLS FOOLS at Ramsey View in Arizona had not known how to reach him … because he had sent his mother his complete itinerary, but it was in the unopened mail! They followed their "policy" to inter their deceased residents in the cemetery there, in the absence of any other directives. In the forms Elise had filled out when she moved there, she had said she would like to be buried next to her husband. Of course, she assumed that Jeff would be around to know what she meant, so she did not spell it out. They did not know where her husband was buried.

Jeff said he had called a couple times from his trip and either got no answer or got a busy signal (as did I when I called!). It never occurred to him that anything might be wrong. And, between us, frankly, Jeff is still too young to have realized just how fragile life is. He bounded off to the South Seas knowing that his lively mother was safe and secure in her new home. When he got home, he called his mother immediately, eager to hear her voice and to say he was coming for a visit. He still could not reach her, so he called the front desk. They were circumspect. They suggested that he phone the health center, who said she was no longer there. He called her apartment again, got no answer, and called the management. They told him that Elise Parker had passed away last week. Ian, what an awful way to learn of the death of a cherished parent. It makes me shiver.

Her Will, Jeff said, is with a Denver attorney, but he does not know which one. He will have to search through her papers at Ramsey View. He can stay at the Ramsey Canyon hummingbird camp, if it is still there. I stayed once at Creek Cabin, to see the migrating hummers, Ian. What has haunted me all these years was a print of the Carolina Parakeet on the wall. It was so bright, so beautiful. But when I looked it up in a book I learned that it has been extinct for a long time. Such a beautiful creature. How tragic that it will never be seen again.

Ian! She is gone. I have before me right now a large packet of letters, my many letters to Elise over these past months. These are letters not opened by the person they were meant for. Never seen by her. A special part of me has died with her. All this time, all these months, I thought she was aware of events that she never knew of. She never met you, she knew nothing of Carson's anorexia, of my newest poems, of the love sent to her in so many forms over so many weeks. How I wish you could have known her.

In writing a letter I send my very soul to those I love. For Elise I was a different soul than I am to anyone, even to you. Aren't we each a different person to everyone else? Don't we each show a slightly different "version" of ourselves to each individual we are with? I know I do. It is even possible that my three children have quite distinct and different ideas of who I really am because of the side of me each sees most often. I do not even act the same around, say, Faye, and Lilla. The "me" that I shared with Elise is now gone forever, torn from me by this sudden and sad news. I had no time to prepare. No time to grieve. It is all already months ago. The news is old. The pain is immediate. Poor, poor Jeff. I know that he feels enormous guilt at not trying more often to reach Elise by phone while he was so far away. Now he has lost her. When he and I talked on the phone, I invited him to stay with me for awhile. But I doubt that he will. He has too many memories of Boulder; it would only sadden him to be here where he grew up. He said he would call me again, with funeral arrangements, etc.

9:45 pm

Ian—I am finishing this hours later. I have had so many phone calls today. The news has gotten around. She had so many friends here in town. I had to phone Emily Evans and postpone our rendezvous. I had a good talk with Alicia. She had called, she said, because of a feeling she had about me. I took a hot bath, had some more tea and a little something to eat, a nap. Where has this long, long day gone? I am so disoriented. It seems as if it has been dark all day outside. I never noticed sun. I will finish this letter tomorrow morning when I have more energy, dearest.

Dawn, March 9————Ian, at this rate I will never get this letter to you completed before I fly out to California. And to think that you are probably there right now, and I can't even reach you! What an irony! I am going to do some laundry, drop Melodie at the vet's, put my answering machine on, and make my travel plans today. Thank Goodness for open-ended plane tickets.

It is only dawn and the Flatirons are already streaked with red and orange against a pale gray sky. This will be a long, long day. Ian, I feel some strength returning as I write you. My atheist acquaintances would ask what the purpose is in believing in God if believing in God cannot strengthen you in a time of trial. It is so true, in a way: in times of shock and grief we sometimes forget to remember that God is the all-knowing Light in the Darkness. And He sent His son to show us that Death is not Victor. I must accept not only this delicate, pastel light of a Boulder morning into my apartment, but the great Light of His Comfort into my soul. Right now. I will copy out just one poem, to share with you, my dear friend, and then I will retreat to the warm kitchen, make a pot of coffee and study my Lesson in the Bible. And as the day evolves, and friends phone, and my plans are made firm, I will emerge carefully from my cocoon and venture out. At dusk I will put my cleats on, so I won't take a bad spill on the black ice, and make my way delicately down the hill, and perhaps take some Shakespeare sonnets with me, and have a hot dinner alone down there amongst strangers in one of the darker taverns. The Bard says this best, Ian. How I wish you were in town so I could lean against you.

SONNET 30

When to the Sessions of sweet silent thought,
I sommon up remembrance of things past,
I sigh the lacke of many a thing I sought,
And with old woes new waile my deare times waste:
Then can I drowne an eye (un-us'd to flow)
For precious friends hid in deaths dateless night,
And weepe a fresh loves long since canceld woe,
And mone th'expence of many a vannisht sight.
Then can I greeve at greevances fore-gon,
And heavily from woe to woe tell ore
The sad account of fore-bemoned mone,
Which I new pay, as if not payd before.
But if the while I thinke on thee (deare friend)
All losses are restord, and sorrowes end.

* * *

March 11

Cat,

As I mentioned on the phone, I have been waiting for Jeff to call with the funeral details. He called last night and told me he's having a memorial service in San Francisco, where

some of Elise's family lives, and where his father is buried.
I had forgotten Bill was buried there. The memorial service
for Bill was here in Boulder last April. Elise's service should
be here, as well, but I don't feel I am in a position to say
that to her only son. It is strange for me to think of Bill's
and Elise's remains over in California. I always associate
them both with Colorado. All of this makes me want to
remind you that when the time comes for me, dear, I would
like to be buried in the spot being saved for me in the
cemetery here, next to your father and little Henry. I know
that you know that, but after seeing the confusion with the
Parker family, I just wanted to remind you to make no
changes. Jeff will eventually have Elise's remains moved
from Monte Vista to San Francisco. But he said that the
paperwork involved could take a long time, and he wants to
have the service now. If you need to reach me, call The
Stanford Court.

Love,

Mother

* * *

Notes to myself for a possible poem

March 19, my birthday

I am a piece of colorful paper. Everyone who knows me
folds me into a different origami shape. The shape for Elise
is gone. The shape for Sam is gone. I must now put a match
to these paper shapes that are not there anymore, except in
my memory, and refold myself entirely for my remaining
days. This loss, of my oldest friend, means that I will
henceforth be different even for my own children, for my
other good friends, and for dear Ian. I need to go to a fair
and stand in front of the mirrors and reflect myself a
thousand times in a thousand images, to prove that I still

am there. A reflection. Death just stole someone from me before I had said all I wanted to say to her, and before she had even read the words I'd been sending since December.

* * *

March 20

Dear Alicia,

I have been home several days, and wanted to thank you for writing to say you had made a memorial donation to the Boulder Public Library in Elise's name. I tried calling you from my hotel before I left, but could reach no one. I talked to Charles once from out there. He and Lilla have their hands full right now with Carson. He said she really wants to come home, return to school, and be left alone. Has the counseling helped? Do you know?

My heart has been so full of late that I have not been much of a parent or a friend to anyone. I missed Faye's anniversary. I think Charles reached Mrs. Allenby one day while I was gone and in their conversation learned about a mugging last month, that I admit I had not told any of you about. He left an acerbic message on my machine about my MOVING!!!! Here we go again.

Wincey made me three meals, froze them, and has been up several times to help me do little chores. She kept Melodie for me, so I did not have to leave her at the vet's, and had a key, which was a godsend. Wincey kept a light on in my home by her quiet love and concern. She understands sudden loss. Each of us, you included, has had our trials. I am coming through this situation better than I had thought I would, and I think it is because, in part, of my focus on spiritual thought. I went to church twice yesterday, maybe because it was my birthday and it seemed a good thing to do.

Dear, treasure your days. Make as much time for David as you can, as I know you already try to. I am here for you, too. Talk to me. I am a good ear. My San Francisco trip, my visit with Jeff, my hours looking out over that vivid city, have brought home to me the need for candor and clarity in all our relationships. That city of hills and vistas does make one face one's interiors. Here in Boulder, looking up at the rock faces of the easternmost waves of the Rockies as they crest across Colorado, I feel a sense of security. The wall of mountains is a comfort to me. San Francisco, on the edge of the great "Pacific" Ocean, is anything but pacific. I am glad to be home.

Alicia, bear with me a while longer. Without Elise to write to, I find myself sharing with you what I would have shared with her. And thank you, thank you, for the beautiful birthday flowers.

love,

mum

* * *

Wednesday, March 22

Dear Faye,

It is a chinook day. It rained yesterday, and washed away the dirty snow. There is a faint sense of spring in the air. I am putting myself back together, like a jig-saw puzzle that got bumped to the floor just as it was being finished at midnight.

As you doubtless know by now, my best pal Elise Parker has died. I asked Charles to phone you to say I had flown to San Francisco for her memorial service. All the letters I'd written her since Thanksgiving were returned to me in a big envelope. It was hard on me, dear. But I am doing better now.

I put some winter things away today, and set out the dhurrie rugs, the Chinese lantern, and the pots of bulbs you sent me recently. The green is starting to show. I made four loaves of currant bread, in the tiny loaf pans, and tied them with white ribbon. I'm going to drop them off later at the doors of the four other widows in this building. I made a special loaf for darling Wincey. She has had a bad cold. One of my friends from here, who now lives in south Florida, has told me how people in her building (she is in an assisted care place) delight in her bringing by little surprises for them at unexpected times. She wrote me not too long ago about what she had planned for some of them for April Fool's Day! Personally, I think she learned to do these fun little surprises and treats from being around me for so long!

Write me when you can, dear.

Love,

Mum

Please forgive my having missed your anniversary! Keep an eye out for a package from UPS.

* * *

Eleanor Bascolm
Editor, Mt. Elbert Press
3124-A Monmouth Street
Denver, CO 80222

Ann C. Bow
Dover Terrace # 10
26 Dover Lane
Boulder, CO 80302

March 29

Dear Ms. Bascolm:

I am writing you because I remember your inquiring about my "religious" writings the last time you and I corresponded. Although I am working on my collection of psalms, for another publisher, I wondered if you might be interested in my poem/prayer/essays. I had sent them to a friend. They were returned to me recently, after her death, and I thought I might send them on to you. I have been in for a few days, what with these chinook winds, and have not felt like braving the sidewalks to reach the bookstore or stationers down the hill, so I am sending you the writings that had been meant for my late friend to read. She was a believer in all things that required a leap of faith. She believed in fairies, the Loch Ness monster, apparitions, and angel messages. I miss her terribly, as she was the one friend in life, aside from my dear, late husband, with whom I could share just about every thought I had. If you read these and find that they are not at all suitable for one of your publishing projects, please return them at your convenience. I would hope, though, that they might be of some real help, real sustenance to a suffering soul. They were products of an Autumn season of work.

I just gave a poetry reading at our local library, and was moved by the response. I needed that positive give-and-take of questions and comments that followed. As a writer, I suppose the same as for all writers, I like to work in my own world, in solitude, but like to share the finished creations with everyone I meet. I am a young spirit, but an elderly lady with an ageless soul in a culture that seems to put less and less value on spirit, ladies, soul, and culture. I do not know how many years, or even months the Lord has for me, and I want to continue with my work, here in my own home, for as long as it is His will. Mine is a simple life, really, with my faith, my books and music, my cat and family, my memories, and the few unrealized dreams still left to fulfill.

I have led a life rich with experiences, complex and lovable people, convoluted and satisfying ideas, and the hope that I have made some small difference. It is in this spirit that I give you these writings. I look forward to hearing from you.

Ann Bow

Feasts

Alone now, you seldom bother
to prepare a regular meal for yourself
anymore.
You often stand in the kitchen,
out of
the one spot
of hot sun and light,
in the shaded corner,
and eat something
straight
from its carton.
        Because you have no
                Special person
                        (husband, parent, or child)
    to cook for or to break bread with,
you have decided that you,
        alone,
are not worth the trouble.
How foolish this is.

You are alone,
as each of us is
ultimately,
since we are alone being born
and alone in our dying,
coming and going in this existence
        by ourselves.
Surrounded by family and friends
        much of your life, you have seen
        yourself as part
                of a group.
But you really are not.
        You are alone.
Accepting your
        aloneness

should not mean that you stop
caring for yourself.
   A small gesture, preparing a meal and
sitting down to enjoy it, in this world
mirrors what we should do for ourselves
       spiritually.

Nourish yourself properly so that you
are filled with the spiritual truths
necessary for survival ... and what might
they be? Faith, honesty, compassion,
truth, love, forgiveness, healing.
You make the list, the recipe.
Take the time, the extra trouble, to
prepare a feast in this wilderness,
to set a spiritual banquet for your
       sustenance,
for the kingdom of God is here now,
and you should learn to
feast therein on the prayers and ideas
God gives you.

*

Repair

Something breaks down: the car, the
washing machine, the furnace. And you
have no one there to fix it. Every time
something breaks down you moan about
the nuisance of it all, about the expense,
the unpredictability, the time wasted
waiting for the repairs to be done.
What must God think about all of us?
So many of us have broken down, have
stopped walking on a spiritual path
toward Him, have fallen in disrepair on

the side of the road. He does not worry
or despair about the time it will take for
us to be mended. He gives us every
chance to right ourselves and to
proceed in our spiritual understanding of
life. You need to pray to be more
patient with the everyday complexities
and repairs of your house, and with the
          everyday complexities of
            spiritual progress.

What good is it, after all, to have the car
repaired if you don't know that the real
                journey
                  is
              Heavenward?

                  *

                Rearing Up

    How difficult and overwhelming it is to
have to rear a child by yourself!
    It requires patience and money and
kindness and hope and
          love.
    You have to provide food, clothes, toys,
education, and
          home.
    You have to be a watchful, careful,
cautious, creative
          conscience.
You help without controlling, suggest without
forcing, and
      guide without pulling.

Isn't this just what God does for us? You must
remember to look to Him for guidance when
you feel baffled as a single parent. Each of us is
His child. How often do we thank Him for the
kingdom of heaven that is our home? How often
do we acknowledge that we are His and He is
                        our Parent,
                            our
                        God?

Each time you button a shirt, pour the cereal,
help with homework, remember that you are not
really a parent alone, but
     a parent with a Parent,
          whose children
          both you and your child are
          now and forever, amen.

                        *

Chores

Endless chores and no one to share them with anymore ....
We are overwhelmed with having to do everything for
     ourselves.
Buy the groceries, carry them inside, put them away.
Cook the food, clear the table, do the dishes.
Buy the sheets, make the bed, do the laundry.
          Turn on the lights, turn off the lights,
               find the electric bill, pay it.
                    The list is
                    endless.

But what are daily chores
but the small, repetitive tasks
     necessary for survival?
Even if we lived alone under the stars

and had no stores or bills we would still need to
    gather, prepare, clean, and secure.
        Chores are reminders.
Each chore
reminds us
that we
depend
on a larger world
for our daily comforts and existence.
        What of our spiritual existence?
        What are its reminders?

Let us remind ourselves through prayer and
        thankfulness
to God that we are dependent on Him
        for our very being.
How often do we remember to thank Him
day and night that we have a day and night,
        food and shelter, ideas and
            friends?

And what chores did Jesus the Christ complete before
    accomplishing his mission on earth
        among us:
loving everyone, sharing his healing work with everyone,
    and promising the kingdom
        of God.
How very small my own daily chores seem compared to his.

*

Storm Preparation

A storm is coming. I should go shopping so that I am
ready
    for days at home
        alone.

I must prepare to provide for myself in case I am stuck in
the house until the roads are cleared. But I dread shopping
with the crowds, with the families buying popcorn and
cookie dough and cider, unworried about loneliness,
because they have each other.
What is it that I must really do? And what is it that I
should really dread? Not the storm, not the shopping, not
the crowds, not being alone.
          Being alone,
I often feel as isolated as a person floating on a raft in a
      stormy ocean.
I seem to have a storm within me most of the time.
          Am I prepared for it?
Do I keep a sampling of rations on hand, so that I can
survive?
          Do I have enough hope right now?
          How about patience and tolerance?
          Am I low in kindness and charity?
          I may be out of wisdom and love.
          I seem to have used so much lately on other people.
          I need to put a warm coat on and venture back
out into daily life to provide for myself the things I need
          most for spiritual survival.
I will replenish the pantry with daily bread:
the knowledge that God is with me all the time
      and provides for my every need: loaves and fishes,
      ever-multiplying love and confidence in the face of
      apparent hunger.
          I need not dread looking for what I need in
the face of a storm.
          The storm can be quelled.
          The larder is stocked now and forever
              with provisions for
              immortality in eternity.

*

Outing

I am going to a park today.
Alone.
I know what to expect there: curving paths, low hills, big
trees, picnic tables, swings and slides,
        and strangers.
    I will pack a small picnic for myself.
A small voice asks me why I would want to go
        to a park for a picnic alone.
    Won't I be saddened to see families there?
    Couples? Happy children?
Why take myself somewhere likely to make me
feel even more alone than I already am?
        I need to rethink the outing.
In the spiritual journey that is my life,
        when I remember to think of it that way,
there are many excursions to quiet places and busy places
        where I must accept that I am alone with my
            thoughts and prayers.
When I select a park for a small outing,
        I really select an oasis set back from the busy traffic
        of everyday.
        I select a time for gentle walking, a light meal, the
        chance to watch strangers playing happily.
        I go where I can sit alone and reflect on the beauty
        around me. I will take a few essentials:
        a loving attitude,
care and concern for my neighbor,
the strength and willingness to meet new people,
and the peace necessary for prayer.
        My daily bread is always with me.
I need but bring it with me, break it, and share it with the
        day.
If I am able to have a spiritual outing every day, I will soon
        walk easily and readily
            with my God.

*

In Touch

I am alone today.
I have no special person with me.
Friends and family are far away.
I could call someone on the phone, or write a long letter.
But days would have to pass before such a letter would
    reach the friend.
And the after-moments of a call feel like a blow,
they can be so lonely.
I need to remember that I am not really alone at all.
I stand not just in an empty room in a house somewhere.
No. I walk in the kingdom of heaven.
Why is it that I am so quick to forget this truth?
Perhaps because the world would as soon it be unknown.
I carry this kingdom within me,
a world within a world within a world,
        a place to retreat to.
Each step during the day is more than a human step
        into a room;
it is a spiritual step towards God.

I am always walking towards Him, and He with me.
    I am on the most important journey of my life.
    I just happen to be walking by myself,
        but not alone,
            not alone,
            today.

* * *

Saturday, April 1 (early)

Dear Wincey,

The sun is just creeping up the mountainside, and it already looks like a clear, bright day! If you see this note early enough this morning (I did not want to phone and awaken you), would you care to join me for a short walk down the Hill for breakfast at "Sunflower's"? I think the fresh air would perk me up. I am sleeping a little better. I still seem to awaken in the middle of the night and have quite a time getting back to sleep. But last night was easier and I feel better this morning. I spent this past week sorting through some of my writings, getting ready to send some work off to a new publisher. I took things from Elise's letters and have put them in a folder. I still find myself reaching for some stationery to drop her a letter.

I think I will try to head to the café by 8:00. Just give me a ring if you get this note in time to join me. If you don't, I will try to catch you today for a cup of coffee up here later!

Ann

* * *

Notes to myself for a poem or essay Sunday, April 2

Every day brings what I call a "sighting," not unlike what Joyce called an "epiphany." A "sighting" is something seen when you are out and around that stuns you with its unexpectedness. It delights. It might be from the world of nature. A "sighting" might be of an owl flying low across a road I am walking beside. It might be a fallen spray of red leaves, catching the day's last ray of sunshine for an instant on a mottled sidewalk. It might be a mysterious little clump of toadstools beneath a tree after a rain. It is the early sun hitting the silver face of my cat and turning her eyes into deep mirrors that reflect my room in two small circles. It is the stag that ran down the mountainside near me, hooves thundering on the frozen ground, and frosty air coming from his nostrils. It is the amber of hot tea in a china cup with circles of light floating briefly in the center.

* * *

Notes to myself, April 4 at "Sunflower's":

More and more, lately, scenes, some funny and some just memorable, pop into my mind and "replay" themselves. This is something new. It is as if memories have come unwound from a spool of film and have begun replaying themselves even when I don't want them to. Is that part of getting older? I seem to be my own "CNN" news broadcaster, reciting the news in a voice almost too low for anyone else to hear, standing someplace near a "breaking" event in my life, microphone in hand, wind blowing my hair.

"Today we learn that God is not central in the life of the Charles Bow family in Columbus, Ohio."

"Last month, Mrs. Samuel Bow of our community was rejected as a volunteer tutor at 'LICENSE FOR LITERACY.' The reason for the rejection was her lack of Spanish."

"This morning was the tenth anniversary of the day that little David Montgomerie, then of San Angelo, Texas, where his father was an instructor in a top-secret, US Security Intelligence Interception Program at Goodfellow Air Force Base, survived his apparent drinking of the entire liquid contents (water, formaldehyde and alcohol) of a 'snow globe' toy that contained a cute scene of Santa and his reindeer on a roof in the snow. His grandmother, who had carelessly handed the baby the toy said she had been out of the room only a minute. And when she returned, she claimed, the snow globe was dry, the crib was dry, and the baby's face had the odor of formaldehyde. Two hours of holding the child in the tub so he could vomit the liquid, after being given an emetic per the Poison Control Center's suggestion, apparently prevented further harm. The child, now 12 and living in Massachusetts with his mother, is doing fine and has no memory of the incident. The grandmother celebrates this 'anniversary' secretly every year by lighting a small candle for the boy and having a moment of prayer."

"Received in today's mail was a Final Will and Testament made by Miss Carson Bow of Columbus, Ohio, sent to her grandmother on floral stationery, in the event she, Carson, were to die soon. No one knows if her parents are aware of this Will."

"Spring is around the corner, and we expect a full day of walking, prayer, worrying, and letter-writing. Stay tuned."

* * *

April 6

Dear Alicia,

I loved the package! And I will write David shortly, but I want you to know that I was delighted with the letter he wrote me the other day. He is developing into a terrific young man. He got the answers to every GrammyAnn Quiz Question, and even added some information on his own, showing me that he had used the library for his work. You should be very proud of him. Thank you for letting me send him a few questions occasionally. Lilla and Charles asked me to stop sending them to Adam, as he just does not have enough time, with his schedule of sports after school, to do anything "extra." I expect you have heard, as I just did, that Carson is home and back at school. The worry now is that her heart has been weakened.

I am so eager to find out which school David would like to attend for his high school years. I would also like to thank you for clearing up my understanding of whether or not you might be moving. I now see that you have to wait until you hear more about your company's new office out here, and that you both have agreed to wait until he starts high school before you make any BIG move. But that is only two years away, and I am thrilled to think you both might want to move West! David's new interest in the Anglican day-school near the Botanical Gardens in Denver certainly was a wonderful surprise, Alicia. It would be more than terrific to have you both so close. These corporate mergers, that I read about so often in the papers, have even affected Bevel and Bevel!

Thank you for asking how I am getting along. Spring is here, although we still have some very cool nights. The students, stripped of their heavy winter parkas and boots, look quite decorative out there in the street in their wild and weird clothes! They seem to move in packs, or flocks, but rarely alone.

I was amazed not to be accepted for a tutoring position. If I were younger I would certainly challenge their denial. I will put it behind me. I do have my work with Common Prayer to occupy any "free" time.

I was walking down Broadway the other day when I saw the most incredible thing, a real "sign of the times." The newspaper calls it a form of "road rage." A funeral cortège was making its way up the street, from one of the big churches downtown, (I actually think it was the funeral for Professor Jacob MacKellar) and several cars that were blocked or delayed started honking impatiently! Then some young men leaned out of a car and actually swore at the people in the lead car! Can you believe it? Have you ever?! This was a first for me. I just felt sick. I never would have expected this here. Maybe in Denver, but not here. "Road rage" is an ugly fact of urban life, I fear. You must have a lot of it around Boston. I see a similar impatience and rudeness here on the Hill just when I stroll down to buy a

New York <u>Times</u> after church on Sunday, and young people rudely take up all the room on the sidewalk, refusing to step aside so I can walk by without stepping off into the street. Amazing. I think it is all part of this giant misunderstanding that all people are "equal," and that no one is expected to be gracious to anyone else anymore. It is part of this awful "hi, guys, what d'ya wanna order" language that waiters use with my friends and me in restaurants! No respect for elders, or anyone, anymore. It makes me shudder. I can just hear my critics now ... what an elitist Ann C. Bow is! But I'm not, dear. Just a classically educated misfit in today's sloppy world.

I have been taking a little walk almost every day lately. I do not feel "cooped up" exactly in my home, but I seem more restless these days, ever since Elise's death. I have not heard from Ian in quite some time. Actually, I have not yet been able to reach him in person to tell him of Elise's death. He has been in California, to help his son and daughter-in-law with their daughter's recent surgery. I hope all has gone well.

Wincey and I have tea, or coffee hour (our own *Kaffee-klatsch*), usually in my living room, at least twice, sometimes three times, a week. I still enjoy little things like grinding coffee beans, baking bread in the bread machine, trying out a new recipe. I have lost a little weight, but have plenty of energy. Melodie has plumped up! She has a happy cat life. That is selfish of me to say, I realize, as the poor dear does not even know, I guess, what she is missing!

I have just sent some essays off to a publisher who called to say she was interested in them. That gives me a good, new project. And the music professor looking through your father's work has found three pieces he would like to submit, with his own notes, for publication, and for performance! Isn't that wonderful? If these pieces *début* out here, and I think they will, possibly at Red Rocks with the Denver Sinfonia, I would LOVE it if all of you children could attend the event.

The three pieces were completed but never named. Professor Jenkins said I could name them, even though he will be "presenting" them to the academic musical world. But I told him I would rather have my three children each name a piece. Would you like to, dear?

Have a good week! Much love,

Mum

* * *

April 10

Dear Em,

Thank you for remembering my birthday. I needed a "pick me up," believe me! I was grateful for the crocheted afghan you'd made me as a surprise! I never learned how to crochet, but am a great admirer of it. I have been lying under it this afternoon, watching the shadows on the Flatirons, listening to cars. I am coming to terms with Elise's death.

I had been counting on Elise to be there for me, selfish as that sounds, I realize. When she lived in Boulder, we saw each other maybe once every week or so, usually meeting at a coffee shop or for a small shopping expedition. But once she moved, I started to write her every few days, as a way to keep her closer, but also as a way to hear myself think. In my own way, I suppose, I was "crocheting" word designs that she could unfold at her leisure and remember me by. I can't tell you how many letters I had sent this fall and winter … but none of them, after mid December, was ever opened or read. A part of me died with her.

I heard an interview, taped years ago, with a famous public figure. She was asked what kept her going through one tragedy after another in her life, and she answered quite movingly, I thought, that her faith was what kept her going. Her losses were so many, and so publicized, that she had to

respond not only to her own grief, but to the world's. I have
had so few losses ... but I would give the same answer: my
faith keeps me strong.

What I find disconcerting is that it seems so very
difficult in this new world we are in, this world of sloppy
language, relaxed morals, excesses in everything from the
enjoyment of pleasure to the infliction of pain, of high crime
and shallow political correctness and cultural misunder-
standings, where the contents of the melting pot seem to
have been dumped into a big blender and put on "whip
until indistinguishable," that it is so difficult to discuss
FAITH! Do you find it odd?

New polls, for whatever they are worth, say that a
majority of our countrymen (am I even "allowed" to use that
term anymore, I wonder) seem to believe in God, and even
in "angels," although "angel" is rarely defined. Yet to sit
down with a friend or new acquaintance, or even your own
grown children, and talk about God, religious views, prayer,
and faith ... well, it seems so hard to do.

I have turned to my own faith in the recent weeks, since
I learned of Elise's death. For some reason, Sam's passing
did not catch me so unprepared. I had not expected him to
die when he did, but I always suspected that I would outlive
him, as he was born eleven years before I was. And he lived
a full, happy life, accomplishing much, dying at the age of
76. Elise, being my own age and settling into a whole new
kind of life at Ramsey View, was ripped from life in a way
that Sam was not. He died in his sleep, you know, with me
beside him. He left with a small whisper of breath, and calm
quiet. The silence is what woke me.

I am so content here, even though I am alone. I don't
know how Sam would have coped with the aloneness, had I
died first. But Elise, like so many older people today, opted to
make a radical move, to change houses. I think she liked the
retirement community, but I'll never really know now. She
was creating a new niche; with a new niche comes something

of a new identity. If I moved from here, especially if I left the area altogether, I would have to recreate myself. Everyone would be a stranger. And, frankly, I am not that interested in redefining myself, especially for total strangers! What would someone think of my daily routines, of early rising and prayerful study, long walks, writing, disinterest in partying? Would a new person ever understand that I prefer reflection and listening to Celtic music to chit-chat and tv talk shows?

Are you planning another trip to Kansas City any time soon? I wanted to ask if you would please go to the gift shop at the Nelson-Atkins Museum, and find me some art post cards from their superb collection. I am making a kind of scrapbook of artistic moments for my granddaughter. She is home from an eating disorders clinic, but not yet fully back in school.

I know I have rambled on and on here ... but I won't ask your forgiveness! I am growing sprouts on my windowsill, trying to have something alive and green in every room. And I have been studying the New Testament, searching for hopes revealed and satisfied. I sometimes wish I had lived then, and could have stepped outside some bright day, to see Jesus walk by with a small crowd. Maybe he would have asked "Who needed my thought just now?" and would have looked over at me in my doorway, and would have smiled, bowing, knowing that we had shared a moment of Truth. I would have bowed, slowly raising my face, to see his eyes, his certainty. My faith, Em, is something I treasure. I nurture it. By the way, if you do get to the Nelson-Atkins, go look at the stunning ivory sculpture called "Fallen Angels."

We need to reschedule your trip up here, if you still have some time. Would you consider coming for Easter? I have no definite plans, except to enjoy an Easter pageant at my church. I would love to have you for a few days. Just let me know. We have nearly two weeks to decide.

I'm off to put your letter in the box, and to throw some goodies into the bread machine so I will have a loaf of

Portugese sweet bread with dinner, as I light a candle, and watch dusk happen to the world beyond. Take care.

Love,

ANNIE

* * *

Friday, April 14

Wincey!

I wondered if you could come up for a little while this evening. I made some *crème brulée* today. It is such a comforting food. I can offer you some sherry or Russian Tea and we can sit in the quiet, and stare out at the stars. I think I need to stare out at stars instead of staring at this world.

I have some news, that came in today's mail, to share with you. It is news which, frankly, caught me totally unprepared. No accompanying or explanatory letter with it, just a traditional, cream card stock announcement with its delicate tissue "veil" over the key words, and a petite, stamped [with that heart "Love" stamp] return envelope, with an unfamiliar Carmel Valley address for the response.

Guess who? Right! Why is it that older widowers almost always choose a young woman, to wed? (Ask me, it is ok, how I know she must be young? Her first name is Tiffany. Very pretty, but my generation tends to associate that with a New York shop.) I suspect they have not known each other very long. He has not spent THAT much time in California lately. Maybe Ian was "struck" by that lightening-bolt thing, as in "The Godfather" where Al Pacino became so infatuated. What would be an appropriate gift, do you think? Perhaps a dust-bunny from the floor, or a fur-ball from the cat, or just silence? If I send nothing, I doubt that I will ever hear from him again. My Edward Steichen book can be taken back to the library now, and I will stop studying art photography. I learned a great deal, but I should stick to my own interests at this stage in my life. I cannot let this news make me ill. I suppose I should wish Ian well. He was a good friend for a brief time. I try to "roll with the punches," as we Americans say. Well, life will go on!

Love,

me

P.S. We can start a new jig-saw puzzle, one I got from Cat for Christmas and have not yet opened. It has 5000 pieces. Perhaps we should do what some old childhood friends of mine do: turn the pieces over to the back so we cannot see the picture! Putting it together really takes skill, then!

* * *

NOTE TO THE READER:

Alicia Bow Montgomerie, now at Bevel & Bevel West, is pleased to share more of her mother's writing.

The Canyon: Poems in a Landscape

Moving On: The Letters of Ann C. Bow to Her Grandchildren

Poems For Patterns: The Fiction of Ann C. Bow

Common Prayers: The Psalms of Ann C. Bow

The Holiday Letters of Ann C. Bow

Psalm/Poem/Essay

Whim and Wisdom: Notes For the Music of Samuel T. Bow

The Havenhome History

Moving Day—The Poems

* * *

The Bow Family

Ann Cunningham born 1926, Jacksonville, Illinois
B.A. In English, Knox College, 1947
M.A. In English, University of Michigan, 1948
Married to Samuel Tremayne Bow, Chicago,
1949

Samuel T. Bow born 1915, Indianapolis, Indiana
B.A. In Music, Northwestern Univ., 1936
Instructor, Univ. Of Michigan, 1936-1941
Lieutenant Colonel, U.S. Army, 1941-45
Assistant professor, Univ. Of Michigan, 1945-54
Professor, University of Colorado, Boulder,
1954-1976
Died, 1991.

Children:

Charles Cunningham Bow, born 1954, Ann Arbor,
Michigan
B.S., 1975, Ohio State University
Married Lillabet Akers, 1984, Akron, Ohio
Carson Bow, born 1986, Columbus, Ohio
Adam Akers Bow, born 1988, Columbus,
Ohio

Alicia Bow Montgomerie, born 1957, Boulder, Colorado
B.A., 1978, Rice University, Houston, Texas
Married David Montgomerie, 1980, Boulder
David Bow Montgomerie, born 1988, San
Angelo, Texas
Alicia divorced, 1991

Henry Tremayne Bow, born 1959, died 1959, Denver,
Colorado

Faye Bow Wills, born 1969, Boulder, Colorado

B.A., University of Florida, Gainesville, 1990

Married Austin Wills, 1990, Boulder

Samuel Tremayne Wills and Cunningham Wills, born January, 2001

— FINIS —